Claim

A Protector Vengeance Dark Mafia Romance

The Carrington Cartel Duet
Book 2

Chiquita Dennie

304 Publishing Company

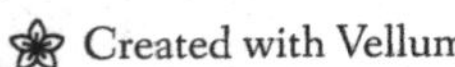 Created with Vellum

Latest Releases

Latest Releases from Chiquita Dennie

    The Early Years-A Prequel Short Story

    Antonio and Sabrina: Struck in Love 1, 2, 3, 4, 5

    Heart of Stone, Book 1 (Emery & Jackson)

    Heart Of Stone Book 1.5 Emery &Jackson A Valentine's Day Short

    Janice and Carlo: Captivated by His Love

    Heart of Stone, Book 2 (Jordan and Damon)

    Temptation

    Heart of Stone, Book 3 (Angela and Brent)

    Cocky Catcher

    Bossy Billionaire

    Bottoms Up Heart of Stone, Book 3.5 (Jessica and Joseph Short

    Love Shorts: A Collection of Short Stories

    Joaquin Fuertes (The Fuertes Cartel Book 1)

    Exposed (Salvation Society Novel)

    Joaquin Fuertes (The Fuertes Cartel Book 2)

    Refuel (A Driven World Novel)

    Pressure (A Driven World Novel)

Until Serena (HEA World Novel)
Antonio and Sabrina: Struck in Love 5
Heart of Stone, Book 4 (Jessica and Joseph)
She's All I Need
Red Light District (A Fantasy Romance Short)
Claim: The Carrington Cartel Book 2
Joaquin Fuertes (The Fuertes Cartel Book 3)
Something Gained (A Romantic Comedy Book 1)
Upcoming Releases (2023/2024):
Fall For You (Satin Hill Book 1)
Dare To Love
Scoring with Sadie
Unveiled (Achille Cartel Book 1)
Nicco: TN Seal Security Book 3
Something Earned (A Romantic Comedy Book 2)

Disclaimer

This work of fiction contains strong language and explicit sexual content and is only intended for mature readers. This story may contain unconventional situations, language, and sexual encounters that may offend some readers. This book is for mature readers (18+).

Introduction

Grab some wine and get ready for more spicy, sinful, sexy suspense.

Are you signed up for my newsletter?

Join today and find out all the latest in new releases, contests, giveaways, sneak peeks and more.

www.chiquitadennie.com

Notes : The Carrington Cartel

Welcome to the Carrington Cartel, a duet series that features characters from Stuck in Love, and Fuertes Cartel. Gigi, Laurent, and Axel briefly appear in the Struck in Love series as an introduction. You do not have to read the entire series, but spoilers are included in this new series. If you want the entire reading order of Struck in Love Universe, check the next page.

Struck In Love Universe
https://books2read.com/u/49Zjnw
Ruthless Struck in Love Book 1
https://books2read.com/u/4AxKLo
Savage Struck in Love Book 2
https://books2read.com/u/bpED6g
Beast Struck in Love Book 3
https://books2read.com/u/3LpgdJ
Janice and Carlo Captivated by His Love
https://books2read.com/u/b6je6M
Brutal Struck in Love Book 4
https://books2read.com/u/4NQyE9
Stolen-The Fuertes Cartel Book 1

https://books2read.com/u/mvZlgV
Saved-The Fuertes Cartel Book 2
https://books2read.com/u/4DWwLd
Redemption Struck in Love Book 5
https://books2read.com/u/b5kZ8O
Betrayed-The Fuertes Cartel Book 3
https://books2read.com/u/4A5LGp
Torn: The Carrington Cartel Book 1
https://books2read.com/u/mqXare
Claim: The Carrington Cartel Book 2
https://books2read.com/u/bwyjPY

Synopsis:

They might have won the first battle, but the war is about to start.

When Gigi and Axel unexpectedly fell in love, the events that followed were expected yet terrible. Turning away from the match her father secured for her to strengthen the cartel left Axel fighting for his life.

Balancing her new role as Boss becomes more complicated than Gigi ever anticipated. But stepping down isn't an option.

Secrets from the past linger in the shadows, and if they come to light, they will destroy everything.

Gigi has always been underestimated, and it's time to show her true wrath and take revenge on her enemies.

Gigi wants blood to pay for what she lost.

Chapter 1

Gigi

Seven months later.

I tossed and turned all night, trying to get a good night's sleep, but nightmares continued to cloud my dreams. The rain descended for the third day in a row, pounding on the roof. Usually, I could sleep if I had Axel next to me, but now it was different.

I felt a kick in my stomach. "Shush," I muttered tiredly. "You decided to keep me company again, huh?"

I turned over, sat up, and stretched my arms over my head. My stomach calmed down a little while I checked the time on my phone. It rang, startling me.

"Yes?" I answered, rubbing my stomach.

"We're outside?" Turin said.

I stood and walked to the window, seeing a few of my men lined up. "All right. I'm on my way down. Give me a few minutes."

Turin blew out a breath. "Boss?"

"Yes, Turin."

"Are you sure you want to do this?"

My eyes stung with tears. "Positive. Please don't question me again."

"Have to look out for you, since he's not here."

My voice was calm. "He would want me to handle business."

"You're right," he responded, amused.

"I'll be down soon."

"No heels this time," he muttered.

I giggled and looked down at my swollen feet. "Let it go, Turin."

"No, because you need someone to watch over you."

"They're only three inches," I teased.

He'd become more of a big brother over the past few months. Our back-and-forth banter was the highlight of my days.

Turin grumbled. "You're determined to drive me crazy."

"As my friend, you should be used to it by now."

"Get dressed." He ended the call.

I shook my head, stood, and walked into the bathroom to shower and dress for another late-night meet-up. The local meat factory had become the destination in order for me to not travel too far during my pregnancy.

Forty minutes later, Turin parked the car in the usual spot and turned toward me.

I frowned. "What?"

He grasped my hand. "The moment I think it's too much, you're leaving."

"Who put you in charge of babysitting me?"

"I put myself in charge. What are the rules again?"

"Turin, I'm fine. Rules are for kids."

The look on his face had me laughing. Most people would think I was crazy pushing a mafia guy around.

"You're pregnant and running a cartel. You need someone to tell you no."

I twisted the ring on my finger and stared off into the night. "That someone isn't here."

"Let's go, so we can get you back home." Turin pushed the door open and rounded the car to help me out.

I stepped out in my long black stretch dress with the split up the right side and three-inch heels. My belly made an appearance before my face. "Is he conscious?"

The guard on duty opened the door to the basement.

Turin held his hand out for me, so I didn't miss a step. "Yeah. I told them to leave you enough to finish him off."

"Thank you."

I scanned the room and took in my surrounding crew as they waited for my orders. I'd reconstructed the Carrington Cartel after what happened with my family and Axel.

"Please, I don't know anything," Sandro pleaded.

I rubbed my belly to calm my baby. "Sandro, I thought we could trust you."

Blood trickled down his face as he lifted his head. Seems they did more than enough damage before I arrived. His clothes were torn, and his wounds were fresh.

"Gigi, I swear Lazaro acted alone!"

My brows pinched together. "Did he?"

"Yes! I can help you, Gigi. Whatever you need."

My frown set into a dark mask. "Dario is missing, and I want his head."

I knew Sandro was lying. I wanted to cut him up into pieces, but we didn't have enough time.

"He's never contacted me," Sandro stated.

"Really? Because I have a phone record that says differently."

Sandro bowed his head.

"Dario is my enemy, and you're going to tell me what you know."

Turin grabbed my arm as I moved in closer.

"Turin, let me go." I stuck my hand in my purse to pull out my gun.

"Gigi, I swear," Sandro whimpered.

"It's Boss to you, Sandro, and I'm afraid you're no longer worth my time."

I pulled the trigger and watched his lifeless body slump. My baby boy kicked up a storm as Turin and I walked out, and our soldiers cleaned up.

I dozed as the music played on the radio and we headed home.

Turin's phone rang, and he pulled it from his pocket. "It's for you."

"Who is this?" I demanded, rubbing my stomach.

"Angel."

I dropped the phone in shock.

"Gigi!" Turin nudged my arm. "You're dreaming again."

I was startled awake as Turin pulled up outside the house. I released a shaky breath and lifted my head toward him. "When is he going to wake up?"

Turin leaned his head on the headrest. "He's fighting for you and the little one in your stomach."

"I keep hoping this is all a dream and the bombing never happened."

Turin's brow creased with worry as he pivoted to face me. "Maybe you should take some time off. Step away from the business, at least until the baby is born."

"No."

His jaw clenched, and his eyes narrowed. "Gigi, I

know you want to prove yourself, but it's getting dangerous."

"Until Dario is found and killed, I won't rest." I reached for the door handle.

Turin's firm hand stopped me. "You know I'm not letting you walk in alone."

"Turin, you worry too much."

"That's my job until my brother comes back."

Turin climbed out of the car and jogged around to my side to help me out. He took the key from my hand and unlocked the door.

I hung my coat on the rack before removing my heels. "You want a drink?"

"No. I need to get some sleep."

"You can sleep in the guestroom. It's late to be driving."

Turin checked the living room and then into the kitchen. This was his routine, and now he had my other guards doing the same thing. When my family was killed in our home in Italy, my protection increased. Turin had become the friend I needed in Axel's absence. Since moving to New York, I'd mostly stayed home unless the girls came and wanted to hang out or I had a business meeting.

I grabbed a bottle of water from the fridge and took a sip as I leaned against the counter. "What?" I asked Turin as he glared at me.

"Put a hold on your plans," he pleaded.

I slowly placed the water bottle on the counter and winced as the baby kicked. "Calm down. Uncle Turin is here," I soothed, rubbing my stomach. I looked at Turin. "I promise I'll think about it."

He placed a hand on my shoulder. "Do more than

think, Gigi. Axel wouldn't want you meeting with his enemies while you're pregnant."

"How will he know?" I asked as I turned and left the kitchen.

Turin shrugged as I reached the stairs. "Because when he wakes up, I'll be the first to tell him."

I laughed. "Snitch."

Turin smirked. "Take it with pride."

I punched him lightly on the shoulder before continuing up the stairs to my bedroom. "You need to find yourself a girlfriend," I yelled and closed my bedroom door.

I heard Turin chuckle as he went to the guest room.

* * *

The next day.

I smiled in the clinical room as the monitor echoed my baby's heartbeat. My days had moved more slowly without Axel in my life, and knowing our baby was growing inside me was the only thing keeping me going.

"Everything is right on track. Have you decided if you want a natural birth without medicine? We're not that far off at eight months," Dr. Noella said, turning off the monitor and cleaning the gel from my stomach.

I sat up and straightened my clothing. "Part of me is scared to go through this for the first time without my parents. I'm eight months along and about to be someone's mom."

Dr. Noella rested a hand on my shoulder. "Did you take my advice and schedule an appointment with a therapist?"

I appreciated Dr. Noella's help, but my problems couldn't be solved with therapy. The only things that would help were my husband waking up from his coma and finding the person who tried to kill him.

* * *

A few minutes later, I left Dr. Noella's private facility after scheduling my next appointment and slipped into the back seat of the waiting car.

"Where to, ma'am?" Ralfie, my driver, asked.

Usually, I would head to the office to look over the books, but my gut told me I needed to see Axel today. "The hospital."

As Ralfie pulled out of the parking lot and made a left down Forty-Eighth Street, nightmarish memories played on repeat in my head. Fulgenzio being blown apart as he started the car, and Axel being thrown back by the blast...

"Ma'am, do you know where you are?"

My eyes felt heavy and my chest was tight. I could barely breathe. "Axel," I whimpered, looking at the stranger. I pushed his hand away as he tried to put an oxygen mask over my face.

"We'll be at the hospital soon. I need you to calm down."

I coughed and tried to sit up, but the EMTs placed me on a stretcher and moved me to an ambulance. Chaos unfolded in front of my home, with the fire department and police surrounding us.

"Where's Axel?" I cried, trying to get out of the ambulance.

"Please try to calm down. Your heart rate is through the roof."

I didn't care about myself. I wanted my husband. "I need Axel."

I glimpsed Axel's lifeless form as they moved him to another ambulance. I reached for him, but darkness dragged me under.

* * *

I blinked my eyes open to a sterile room. Tubes ran from my arm and oxygen hissed at my nose. Janice and Sabrina stood in the corner, talking to a nurse. I glanced toward the window and saw Turin. My throat was dry. I tried to clear it but only made it worse.

"Axel," I whispered.

Everybody scrambled to my side.

Sabrina gripped my hand, and Janice smoothed my hair off my face.

"Where's Axel?" I croaked.

Janice and Sabrina shared a look.

"Turin, where is Axel?" I demanded, my voice stronger.

Turin rubbed the back of his neck, dipping his head to avoid my glare.

"Gigi, you need to relax," Janice said calmly.

Something was wrong. They were trying not to upset me. I snatched the wires out of my arm and the nurse hit a button to call for the doctor.

"Mrs. Carrington, I need you to relax and take deep breaths," she encouraged.

I didn't care what she needed because I needed my husband. "Is he dead, Turin? Tell me, please!" A tear tracked down my cheek. I'd lost so much already and to have the best thing that had ever happened to me taken away would undo me forever.

Turin lifted my chin and looked into my eyes. "He's alive."

"Thank god!"

"But he's in a coma," he continued. "And they're not sure if he'll ever wake up."

I gasped and my chest tightened. "I can't breathe."

"I told you we should've waited." Janice focused on me as more nurses and doctors burst through the door.

"Clear the room!" the doctor shouted as my eyes rolled to the back of my head.

The next day, I found out I was pregnant.

* * *

Once we arrived at the hospital and parked in the visitor's section, it didn't take long to get checked in. Ralfie let the other guests step off of the elevator and motioned that it was safe. I slipped off my shades as we rode the elevator to Axel's private room. The blinds were open. I figured the nurses must have changed his sheets and left them open for him. He looked like he was sleeping peacefully and could wake up at any moment.

I placed my purse and glasses on the chair, removed my coat, and leaned forward to kiss his forehead and then lips. I caressed his cheek. "Time to wake up, baby."

Axel was the one who reassured me, and I felt confident and safe in his world. It was my turn to reassure him and show that I could protect our family now that he was the one who was hurt.

I rubbed his arm. "Turin and I are close to finding him."

The monitors beeped.

I ran a hand across his chest and up to his full beard.

His brows were bushy and thick. "Soon as you get out of here, we'll get you a fresh cut and trim your beard. You know it itches when you kiss me." I laughed softly, and the monitor beeped faster. The doctors had told me that people in comas could hear you and feel your presence.

"We know nothing in life is easy, but I could use your love right now. That was always easy." Remembering the warmth of his smile made me feel like his arms were around me.

The door opened and Trina, one of the nurses, came in. She was in her late forties and had come recommended by Janice. She knew how to be discreet.

"Any changes?" I asked as she wrote on the whiteboard.

"Not yet, honey, but the more you visit and talk, the more it helps," Nurse Trina explained with a smile.

"Hope so."

Her smile grew. "How are you feeling? You're going to be a mommy soon."

The monitors went crazy.

"What's happening?" I panicked and reached out to rub Axel's forehead.

Trina gripped my shoulders. "Gigi, step outside for me."

"No! Tell me what's going on?"

Trina lowered Axel's bed as more nurses and doctors came into the room. "Get her out of here!" she yelled.

Nausea clawed up my throat. He wasn't going to make it, and we'd be all alone in this world. More staff piled in as I was led from the room. I held a hand over my heart and mumbled a prayer to God to keep Axel safe. My life had just started to make sense with him. My confidence in his recovery was fading.

Chapter 2

Gigi

The doctors later explained that Axel was going to be fine and for me to get some rest, but I refused to leave his side. Hours rolled by, so I lay on the couch to grab some sleep.

"Gigi! Gigi!"

Someone nudged me, and I woke with a jump. My gaze flew to Axel, and I sighed in relief to see him still in bed.

"When was the last time you ate?" Turin demanded.

His chiding tone made me angry. "What are you doing here?"

He shook his head. "Don't deflect the question."

I sucked in a breath and rolled my eyes. "Probably this morning."

"Probably? Gigi, you know Axel would be livid that you're not taking care of yourself."

"Who told you I was here?" I asked, ignoring his statement.

Turin looked at Axel. "Ralfie called me once the nurses got things under control with Axel."

"Remind me to fire him," I sassed as I stood and stretched.

"We got a possible hit on Dario," Turin stated.

I spun to face him. "Why didn't you say that first?"

"You've been through a lot, Gigi. I know you feel like everything is on your shoulders, but let me help," Turin pleaded.

He was right. I held a lot of things close to my chest because my trust was shot after what Dario and Lazaro had done. "What do you have?"

He stroked his chin. "It's in Chicago."

I watched him intensely. "Chicago."

Turin stepped to Axel's bed and stared at his best friend. "A few contacts told me that Igor Mendoza might be doing business with the Ramini family." His lips pressed into a disapproving line.

My ears perked up. "Since when?"

The Mendoza Cartel had a long-standing deal with our family, plus the De Lucas made it clear they wouldn't work with anyone who supported Dario or his family.

"Dario shouldn't be underestimated. We made that mistake before. He had to have made contingency plans." I slid my feet into my heels. "Get the jet ready to leave first thing tomorrow."

Turin grimaced. "I can handle Igor alone."

"Turin, we've had this conversation too many times."

He motioned to my stomach. "That was before you were eight months pregnant."

"You'll be with me, and so will Ralfie. Igor would be stupid to do anything to a pregnant woman."

"Sometimes that naivety won't work."

"That's what I'm counting on."

He sighed. "Shouldn't you be resting and preparing for the baby?"

I ignored Turin's comment and scooped up my things. I kissed Axel goodbye and left the hospital with Turin and Ralfie.

* * *

Turin was right. I should take more time to enjoy my pregnancy. I decided to call the girls over that night before we headed to Chicago to handle Igor. Even though I couldn't drink, I made sure they had more than enough alcohol to enjoy themselves, plus food.

The doorbell rang as I popped a strawberry into my mouth. I slid off the bar stool and sauntered to the door while the chef continued to set up the food. Lately, the business took a front-row seat, and my self-care was lacking, even though I stayed on top of my doctor's visits. Knowing Dario was still out there made it difficult for me to fully embrace my pregnancy because all I wanted was revenge.

I opened the door, and Janice held up two bottles of champagne. I stepped aside to allow her and Sabrina to enter, shaking my head at her goofiness.

"You know I can't drink." I pouted as I grabbed one of the bottles and checked the label.

"Apple cider. We can fake it until you drop," Janice joked.

I chuckled, waving them into the kitchen. "Chef Ebony, you remember my friends, Janice and Sabrina, from the funeral?"

Months ago, after the incident, I had a small gathering

to honor Fulgenzio. Chef Ebony took care of the entire meal without complaints and even handled the cleanup.

"Nice to meet you ladies again, and please call me Ebony," she said with a smile.

Janice picked up a plate and filled it with pancakes, French toast, casserole, fruit, scrambled eggs, and grits. Another thing I'd learned with my new life in America was not to worry about my size. It was freeing because my mother had always tried to make me skinny like a model to attract a husband. Trying different foods and having a chef was fun because I could have whatever I wanted—a blessing considering the cravings that came with being pregnant. No longer did I have to be picky, but I made sure to balance healthy days with splurge days, especially now I was eating for two.

"Come on and eat in the dining room." I grabbed hot tea and my food.

Janice sat across from me, and Sabrina sat beside me at the head of the table.

Sabrina poured a glass of juice. "Antonio told us you and Turin might be close to finding Dario."

Any mention of Dario made me anxious and caused my blood pressure to rise. I took a sip of my drink. "Yes. I have to fly to Chicago tomorrow."

Sabrina and Janice looked at each other, then eyed me. In two seconds, the questions would start.

Janice dabbed her mouth with her napkin and cleared her throat. "Chicago? For what?"

I placed my fork on the table. "A potential lead on Dario."

"Have you thought about leaving this alone? Or at least wait until the baby is born and Axel wakes up."

I huffed. Janice and Sabrina had taken things into their own hands several times. "No, he has to pay now."

"What about Axel's condition?" Sabrina inquired.

My chest throbbed with pain. "Axel would want me to do this for him."

"Not true, Gigi. Axel made it his business to keep you out of trouble," Janice pointed out.

She was right, to some extent. At the beginning of our relationship, Axel didn't like me being in the cartel, but when I became the Boss, he supported my decisions. "You had family and your husband's backing. I'm alone."

Sabrina jumped up and wrapped her arms around me. "You will never be alone, Gigi. I promise. We're here for you." She wiped the tears from my eyes with her napkin.

I fanned myself to calm the flow of tears. "Did Carlo and Antonio do a good job of keeping you two out of trouble?"

Sabrina nodded as she sat down.

"I need you to support my decisions," I stated, looking between them.

"Whatever you need, we'll help," Janice said, placing her hand on top of mine.

I smiled and squeezed her hand. "Thank you."

"So, tell us about Chicago. Who are you meeting?" Sabrina asked.

"Have you heard of the Mendoza Cartel?"

Janice gave me a knowing look. "Carlo has talked about them before."

"I need to make a good impression."

Janice grinned. "I think meeting a very pregnant Boss will make an impression."

I smiled and rubbed my stomach. "My secret weapon."

Janice and Sabrina looked perplexed but didn't say anything.

We finished eating and watched a movie in the theater before it got too late, and they headed home to their families. Tonight had helped to clear my mind and feel normal, if only for a little while.

* * *

After a good sleep, I showered and listened to old-school love songs, thinking of Axel as I got ready for the day.

The plane journey passed quickly, and before I knew it, we were landing in Chicago. My driver was waiting with a fur coat which I wrapped around my shoulders to keep the winter chill at bay. I wasn't sure why we needed to meet with the Mendoza Cartel on such short notice, but I figured it was a test to see if they could trust me.

The strip club doors opened, and the guard reached for me to check for weapons.

I stepped back in annoyance. "I don't think so."

He sneered at me. "It's the rules."

"Tell your boss I don't follow the rules."

I heard a chuckle as men approached us in the hallway. "Gigi Carrington." Igor Mendoza extended a hand.

I needed to put on a brave face and not show any sign of weakness. "Tell your men to back off."

Igor regarded me cooly. "No offense, but everybody gets checked in my presence."

"Offense taken. I came to talk business. I have no reason to carry a gun and am no threat to you."

He stared at me for a long moment before nodding for

me to pass. I smirked at his bodyguard and followed Igor with my guard behind me. My heels clicked against the floor as we approached a tall steel door.

Igor opened it and indicated I should precede him, but he stopped my guard at the door. His gaze moved to me. "Only you."

"Are you scared, Igor?" I challenged him.

He grunted and shut the door behind him.

I took a seat and crossed my legs as I watched him pace around the table. "You're making me nervous, Igor."

"I got a call to meet with the daughter of Laurent Carrington, and she came. Would make any man nervous." Igor sat on the edge of the table in front of me. He reached out and gently caressed my cheek.

I slapped his hand away. "Don't touch me."

"Aren't you scared I'll do something to you?"

I grinned and leaned forward so our lips were an inch apart. Slipping my hand beneath my dress, I pulled out my small pistol.

The smile dropped from his face.

"Here's the problem, Igor. All men are the same, and you've proven how stupid you are to fall for a pretty face."

"You won't get away with this," he sneered.

I chuckled. "I'm not killing you. Today, Igor, you will do what I want."

His brow hiked. "And if I don't?"

"While you were allowing me to come in without getting a pat down, my men were surrounding the building. Every dancer, bouncer, and customer will die, and the blame lies with the Mendoza Mafia family. What do you think the news will say about you?"

He clenched his teeth. "What do you want?"

I smiled and gently tapped him on the cheek with the gun. "You work for me now."

"Bullshit!" A belligerent and inflamed curse escaped his lips.

"Oh, is the big bad bully mad?" I stood and gripped his chin.

The Mendoza Cartel had run Chicago for years, so to have me come in and take over was crippling to his ego. My plan to dominate and weed out the snakes started now, and Igor would help me.

"Either you realize I have you by the balls, or the police would love to investigate how an entire strip club blew up with the owner inside over a drug deal that ended badly," I explained. I placed the gun back under my dress and headed for the door.

"How much?"

I looked back at him. "Your percentage would be fifteen. I'm feeling generous."

His anger became a scalding fury. "Bitch! My men would look at me like a fool for fifteen percent."

"I'm willing to negotiate, but since you want to call me a bitch... Five percent sounds good to me." I pulled the door open and motioned to my men for us to leave as Igor yelled and cursed.

"How did it work out?" Ralfie asked.

"Keep walking," I muttered, wanting to get out of the building as quickly as possible.

Igor didn't need to know that I'd lied about having explosives set up. I could almost hear Axel now, pissed that I'd taken a chance with another powerful family by blackmailing them to get what I wanted.

We finally made it back to the hotel I'd reserved for the two-day trip. I told my guards we'd leave tomorrow and to make sure the pilot was ready to take off on time. My priority was checking in on Axel at the hospital.

My phone rang and Turin's name flashed on the screen. I grabbed a bottle of water from the fridge as I answered. "Yes, Turin."

"You think it was a wise move to threaten Mendoza?"

"He's on board, isn't he?"

"Gigi, that's not how things work," he hissed.

"In my world, they do," I responded sharply.

"All you did was buy him time to come up with another alternative."

I sauntered into the bathroom and turned on the shower, scanning my face in the mirror. The bags under my eyes were becoming more prominent.

"Turin, what's done is done. Either you're on board or you're not, but wasting time arguing won't change my answer."

Silence greeted me on the other end.

"Hello?"

"I went to see Axel today."

I closed my eyes. "Did he wake up?"

Turin's voice was low. "No."

Steam fogged the bathroom. "I'll call you tomorrow on the flight back."

Before he could respond, I ended the call. I dropped the phone on the counter and gripped the edge, taking deep breaths. My little guy could feel the tension and knew my energy was off.

"It's okay, Peanut. Mommy's fine."

I released another breath before undressing and stepping into the shower. Twenty minutes later, clean and refreshed, I ordered food from room service and climbed into bed to watch a movie.

* * *

I woke to a presence around me, like someone watching me when a familiar gritty voice caused my heart to race.

"I was going to give you another two minutes before I woke you up."

I reached over and turned on the lamp. Igor was sitting in the chair beside the bed. "How did you get in here?"

Igor ignored my question. "Nice trick you pulled earlier?"

"How did you get into my hotel room?" I demanded in a shrill voice.

Igor boasted. "Someone owed me a favor. This is my town, Princess."

I reached under the pillow and cursed under my breath.

Igor held up my pistol. "Is this what you're looking for?"

I leaned against the headboard, feigning a calmness I didn't feel. "What do you want, Igor?"

"You played me earlier today, Princess." His voice was bitter.

I tilted my head. "It was business."

Igor caressed the gun between his fingers.

"Don't even think about killing me. I can assure you the second you walk out, you're dead."

His eyes pierced the distance between us. "Dario told me how feisty are."

My mouth was set in a stubborn line. "Did he also tell you how easily I could have you killed?"

His mouth twisted wryly. "That doesn't scare me, Princess."

"Stop calling me that!"

He laughed, and I wanted to wring his neck. Axel taught me to not lose my composure, but Igor had me in a vulnerable situation.

"The proposal is, how do you Americans say? Null and void."

"Like hell it is!"

He rose from his seat. "New terms for you."

"And if I don't agree?"

He pointed a finger at my stomach.

"Igor, you're swimming in dangerous waters, my friend."

Igor smirked and stepped toward the bed. I kicked out and reached for the phone, but he smacked it off the nightstand and gripped the back of my head. "Bitch! I'm the Boss of this city!"

I tried to keep my body covered while yanking his fingers from my hair. Suddenly, the door flew open, and Igor's eyes widened as Turin burst in with two of my men, their guns drawn.

Igor tried to pull me in front of him as leverage, but I punched him in the balls and crawled across the bed.

"Fuck!" he roared, just as Turin fired a shot into his leg.

I grabbed my robe and tightened it around my body to cover my nightgown.

"Are you hurt?" Turin asked.

I waved him off. "I'm fine. Give me the gun."

"Gigi—"

"Now!" I was tired of people telling me what to do and how to behave.

Turin handed me the gun, and I walked around the

bed. Igor was squirming on the floor, clutching his leg. I raised the gun to his face.

"Kill me and you'll never find Dario," he seethed.

"That's a risk I'm willing to take."

"My family will seek revenge."

"The Mendoza Cartel is more than welcome to come see me. I'm not running, motherfucker." I pulled the trigger.

Turin took the gun from me. "We need to get out of here." He moved to the window to check the area.

"Let me get--" I paused and bent over the bed when I felt a sharp pain.

"What's wrong? Gigi, is it the baby?"

I winced. "I'm fine."

Turin ran off orders to the other men. "Clean this up and pay off the hotel staff. Get the security footage from the past three days."

Finally, the sharp pains stopped, and I headed to the bathroom to get dressed.

"I'm taking you to the hospital." Turin said as we piled into the car five minutes later.

"Turin, please. It's been a long day."

"You're the Boss of them, not me," Turin said, motioning to my men. "If Axel were here, he'd be pissed."

"But he's not!" I yelled, angry that I let my guard down.

I knew Turin was right, but everything had happened so fast. I just wanted to be with Axel like it was in the beginning.

"You need to be hundred percent when he wakes up. Focus on you and the baby. Dario isn't going anywhere."

I turned to stare out the window as we headed for the hospital.

An hour later, I was resting in a hospital bed while my and the baby's vitals were monitored. Turin stood in the corner talking with Ralfie.

The door opened, and a doctor arrived with a nurse.

"Is everything okay with my baby?" I asked immediately.

"Everything is fine, Mrs. Carrington," the doctor replied, looking at the folder in his hand.

"Then I can leave?"

The doctor looked at his nurse, then back at me with a serious expression. "I'd advise you to stay here for the next few days as a precaution so we can monitor you and the baby."

"But I thought you said the baby is fine."

"He's perfectly healthy, but based on you traveling on such short notice and having pains..."

I glared at Turin for revealing my personal business. Returning my gaze to the doctor, I asked, "Can I fly back home, yes or no?"

"I talked with your doctor and she said you can fly home, but you'll be on bed rest if anything else comes up."

"Great. Please send me the discharge papers."

"Sure, but first, let the nurse check your vitals one more time."

I thanked the doctor as he left the room, along with Turin and Ralfie. I allowed the nurse to look me over and then relaxed in the bed in deep thought once she left me alone.

"Mommy will protect you, Peanut." I leaned my head back on the pillow and forced myself to eat the hospital food.

* * *

As the plane lifted off for New York, all I had to show from our time in Chicago was a dead body. Dario was still on the run, and I was probably going to be put on bed rest if I didn't slow down on my manhunt. Turin, Janice, Sabrina, and Dr. Noella were pushing me to focus on my health.

"Mrs. Carrington, would you like something to drink?" the flight attendant asked with a tray full of my favorites.

"No, thank you. I'm going to take a nap in the bedroom," I replied with a smile. I turned to Turin. "Wake me when we land."

Turin nodded and continued to work on his computer. Ralfie was asleep in the chair. I locked the door behind me and slid under the covers, dozing off to my favorite dream of Axel and me with our son.

When the plane landed, we climbed into the bullet-proof cars and left the airstrip. As usual, Turin and Ralfie checked the house on our return. I left them to do any check-in with security and climbed into bed in one of Axel's shirts. If he were here, he'd have an arm wrapped around me and his face buried in my neck, whispering how much he loved me. That always put a smile on my face when going to sleep.

Chapter 3

Axel

A month later.

"So how many kids do you want?" Gigi asked.

"None," I replied.

"You can't be serious, Axel." Her hands landed on her hips.

"I'm very serious, Gigi. I told you, I'm not your friend."

"How many times are you going to pretend you don't like me?"

I'd let my guard down a few times with her, and tonight she'd skipped out on her parents' party to hide at the lake. Laurent threw lavish parties all the time to close deals. Tonight, some of his most trusted associates would be there and, I figured, a few enemies.

Gigi stuck her feet in the water. Her metallic-gold dress clung to her curves. "My personal life has nothing to do with you." She turned to look at me with a grin. "Axel, are you scared of my questions or your attraction to me?"

I stood my ground. "None of the above."

"Then why are you out here?"

"Because I was asked to keep an eye on you."

Gigi flicked the water with her feet and giggled. "No one is going to bother me in my parents' home."

"Sounds like a spoiled princess."

Gigi inclined her head back. "Excuse me, I work very hard."

"Sure you do."

She faced me and planted her hands on her hips.

I knew what she was about to do would piss me off. "If you even try it..." I threatened.

"What are you going to do?" Gigi raised her leg high and before she could send a splash of water, I stepped back a few feet.

"Gigi!" her mother called, heading toward us.

"What?" Gigi shouted.

"Have you lost the small amount of dignity we instilled in you?" Her mother marched to the edge of the water.

Gigi always looked vulnerable when her mother was around. "I needed a break."

"Break's over. Come back inside," Rosa demanded.

"Why?" Gigi whined.

"Because Dario is looking for you."

"Fuck Dario," she mumbled.

Rosa's voice rose an octave. "What did you say?"

"Nothing, Mother." Gigi strolled out of the water in a huff as her mother whirled and stalked back to the house.

Gigi turned to me. "Your first child will be a boy."

I followed a few feet behind her as she walked back to the house. "What makes you say that?"

She stopped walking and stared at me. "Because you seem like the type who would be a Girl Dad, and I want to be the only woman you spoil."

The long-forgotten memory replayed in my head and tugged at my heart. I flinched at the pain in my chest. The door opened, and I glanced at the short woman who entered the room.

Her eyes widened as she approached the bed. "Mr. Bresciani! You've finally come back to us. We were worried you'd never wake up."

I tried to lift my hand, but it wouldn't move.

"Just relax. I'm going to call the doctor." She pressed the call button and checked my chart.

I opened my mouth to speak, but something obstructed my throat. I reached for the tube in my mouth.

"I'll take it out soon as the doctor arrives," the nurse assured me.

A few moments later, the doctor came in with another nurse. I was used to being in control, but I was currently at the mercy of others. I'd promised myself I'd never depend on anybody after my parents' death.

I scanned the name on the doctor's white coat as he directed the nurse with the red-haired to check my feet and legs.

He wasn't more than five-seven, with glasses and gray streaks in his hair. "Mr. Bresciani, welcome back. I'm Doctor Nathaniel."

I pointed again at the tube in my throat, and he checked my pulse before removing it. The minute it was gone, I felt relief. I tried to speak, but my voice was raspy and hollow.

"Here, drink some water. It'll help," the nurse explained.

I took a sip. "When did I get here?"

"Sir, you've been here for several months," Dr. Nathaniel informed me.

"What happened?"

"A car explosion from what the police said. They've been waiting for you to wake up to talk with you and your wife."

My wife.

"Do you know where you are?"

"New York."

Dr. Nathaniel nodded. "Good. And your wife's name?"

My voice was raspy and my throat was dry. "Gigi."

"Excellent. We'll contact her as soon as we run more tests."

Every muscle went rigid. "Is she all right?"

"Do you remember what happened to you that night?" Dr. Nathaniel folded his hands in front of him.

"I remember leaving my house after talking to my wife. I was with Fulgenzio."

Dr. Nathaniel exchanged a somber look with the nurse. "Unfortunately, your friend didn't make it."

"Fulgenzio is dead?" I whispered.

Dr. Nathaniel nodded. "I'm sorry. As soon as we run some more tests, we'll call your wife."

Fulgenzio was young, with a long life ahead of him. There was a new pain in my heart that my wife wasn't here with me. I had so many dreams of us together and happy. "But is she okay?"

"Your wife is fine, sir. You'll see her soon."

Evidently, there was more to the situation, but they

avoided my questions. I frowned when the door opened again, and in walked my best friend and a man I considered a brother.

Turin's face was marked with new lines. "Axel, you're awake! I just came to check in on you."

I didn't wait for the nurse to change the bandage on my stomach. "Where's Gigi?"

"Is he alright, Doc?" Turin avoided my question.

"Tell me, Turin." I needed to get out of here. Something was going on with Gigi, and everybody knew except me. I turned to the doctor. "Discharge me."

"Sir, you've just woken from a coma," Dr. Nathaniel reminded me.

I pushed the covers back and tried to get out of bed, but exhaustion engulfed me. I needed my wife.

The nurse tugged on my arm to keep me in bed. "Sir, you can't leave yet."

"Discharge me or I'm leaving anyway," I growled as beads of sweat trickled down my face.

"Axel, she's in labor. I just got the call," Turin finally answered my question.

I tried to lunge at him for betraying me, but he was too strong and pressed me back on the bed.

"Calm the fuck down. It's me, your best friend."

"She's pregnant," I grumbled. I felt empty and nauseated.

He gripped my arms. "It's your baby, you stupid motherfucker. Relax and let the doctors finish, and I'll wheel you up there."

"Get the fuck off me!" I shouted.

He backed up.

Did I believe he betrayed me? No. But I'd had enough

lies and betrayal over the past few years not to trust even my closest people.

Doctor Nathaniel continued with his exam and checked my eyes, ears, and legs. He decided I would be okay to go to Gigi's room, but he wanted me back in bed soon.

Turin pushed me in the wheelchair up to the labor and delivery area. He explained that Gigi had a private floor, considering our enemies were still lingering. I was grateful to him for being here to help her in my absence.

We arrived at her door, where two guards were stationed. They straightened when they saw me, and their eyes widened as if they'd seen a ghost.

"Run down everything that happened," I demanded.

"We can talk about it afterward."

"Turin, I need answers." The ache in my chest almost exploded with panic.

He rocked on his feet and ran a hand down his face. "You remember me coming to get you that night we had a hit on Dario?"

"It was late. I told Gigi I wouldn't be out long, and I kissed her goodnight."

"It happened before I got there, but Gigi said you were caught in the explosion."

"Was she hurt?"

"No, but she was shaken up. Remember, she'll be all over the place. She's in labor."

"I'm a father."

"Yeah, so stay calm."

"What do you mean?"

"There are things we can discuss when you leave here."

I swallowed the lump in my throat. I'd left Gigi for so long to deal with so much stress.

Turin opened the door and wheeled me inside. We both froze.

Janice and Sabrina stood at the side of the bed as Gigi slept. A gasp left Janice's mouth.

"We thought you were still in a coma," Sabrina said, her eyes wide.

My mouth was dry and my stomach was tight. "I woke a little while ago. Is that—"

Janice came around the bed with the baby in her arms and held him out to me.

I shook my head. "Not yet."

"Axel, it's your son," Janice said softly.

I cleared my throat. "Afraid I might drop him."

Janice raised her eyebrows and handed him to me. She helped me to support his head properly and rolled my wheelchair next to Gigi's bed.

"She's been sleeping for a while," Sabrina added from where she sat on the couch near the window.

I brushed a finger across my son's cheek. "Can you give us a few minutes?"

Janice, Sabrina, and Turin all looked at each other.

"Okay, we'll be right outside if you need anything or the baby gets fussy," Janice said.

My gaze dropped to my son. His eyes were closed. Never did I imagine being a husband, let alone a father. Everything I thought made me weak or broken disappeared the second I looked at him. Gigi and my son made me stronger and wiser. Dario might have lit the match, but I controlled the flames.

A small voice whispered. "Axel?"

Gigi extended her hand to me. I took it, kissing her palm before holding it to my cheek and then my heart.

My eyes darted toward our son. "You scared me."

Gigi winced when she tried to sit up. "That makes two of us."

Slowly, I lifted him up to her. "He looks just like you."

She yawned. "Wish you were with me."

"I can't apologize enough for missing our son's birth."

She reached over and tilted my chin up. "Never blame yourself."

"What's his name?"

"I wanted to wait for you, but Sabrina and Janice thought it would be a good idea to give him an identity before we left the hospital if you didn't wake up."

"They're right."

For the rest of my life, I would show my son how much I loved him and his mom. I wanted another child already, though I knew it was bad timing to bring it up. "He's going to need a sister or brother soon."

Gigi chuckled and shook her head.

My attention went to my son as he started to feed. Something so simple yet so beautiful.

Gigi smiled down at him. "Axel, meet your son, Gaspare Laurent Bresciani."

"You named him after my father."

Gigi rocked him back and forth. "Thought it would honor both our fathers. Is that too much?"

Her words tugged at my heart. Nobody imagined Gigi and me together. Our personalities were so different, and she was young when we met.

Now I'm her husband.

Now we have a son.

And I'll do whatever it takes to protect my family.

* * *

After spending time with Gigi and my son, the nurse wanted to take him to get cleaned up, and Gigi needed her rest. Turin wheeled me back to my room to pack up my things. I'd decided to go home, even without the doctor's permission, to recover in my own space.

Doctor Nathaniel tried to persuade me to stay in the hospital a little longer, but I ignored his requests and set Turin in charge of putting what I needed in my home for me to get better. I felt too vulnerable at the hospital, knowing that Dario could get to my family. Whoever was helping Dario would do anything to get to us, and I wasn't strong enough to fight anyone—yet.

I sat in the chair beside the bed and looked at Turin. "I've been here for months. What happened with Dario?"

"I wanted to wait until you both came out of the hospital."

"Turin, I can take it, whatever you have to say."

"For at least seven months, I've tried to keep Gigi clear-headed, but she's taken things too far."

My eyebrows knitted together. "How?"

"The Mendoza Cartel."

The Mendozas weren't necessarily our enemies, but they were closer to the Ramini family than us, even though we'd done business together. "What happened?"

"We may have bigger problems besides Dario."

I sat up straight. "As in Hugo?"

"We killed Igor Mendoza."

My brow hiked. "We?"

"A tip came through that Dario made it here from

Italy because of Igor Mendoza. I checked it out, and it's true based on the flight schedule." Turin pulled up his phone and explained how our tech team tracked phone records of Dario and Casella's men who worked with the Mendoza Cartel. The flight manifest of a private jet showed one person on board fitting Dario's description.

I was sure Gigi's actions were warranted, but killing Igor Mendoza would cause a bigger fight that we weren't fully prepared to handle. "How did you let this happen?"

"You know better than me how stubborn Gigi is when her mind is made up."

"She was pregnant!" I bellowed. "You should have controlled the situation."

"Each step she took became more complicated and sometimes she went alone."

That's why Gigi needed to step down and put Turin or someone else in charge while we both recovered. The thought of Gigi and our unborn child in danger pissed me off, and she knew I would be infuriated at her for trying to chase Dario down.

"Something else you should know."

"What?"

Turin grabbed the rest of my things and dropped them in the bag. "Gigi's mother is behind your parents' death. She had help from Edmundo."

My jaw clenched. "She's lucky she's dead."

My son, with his dark brown eyes, short curly hair, and golden-brown skin, was the only thing keeping me sane. He and his mother.

* * *

Turin brought the car around while the nurse pushed the wheelchair to the SUV and helped me climb in.

Janice stood by with her arms crossed and a scowl on her face, pissed that I'd decided to check myself out against the doctor's orders. "Gigi is going to be pissed when she finds out."

"She'll be fine. I'll call and check up on her in a few hours."

"Axel, are you sure about leaving?" Sabrina asked.

"I need to be home to work on getting better. Being here keeps me paranoid."

"Antonio will want to hear from you." Sabrina studied my face in the light.

"I'll call him when I make it home."

Turin shut the door and hurried around to the driver's side. As we left the parking structure of the hospital, he passed me a new phone and gun. I had to get back in shape as soon as possible because Dario partnering with Mendoza would impact my family's safety.

Chapter 4

Gigi

A few hours earlier.

"I want the baby's toys in that closet over there," I directed my staff while Janice and Sabrina helped me carry in the shopping bags.

Since returning from Chicago, I'd listened to my body and relaxed my efforts to find Dario until after the baby was born. Turin ignored me on the plane, all the while making sure he paid off the right people to get the security footage removed. Killing Igor was a mistake, but not something I regretted because it was him or me.

I separated the baby clothes into different piles and made sure I checked off my list of last-minute items I'd need for a newborn.

"Gigi?" Janice called.

I left the bedroom and walked to the hallway to peer over the balcony. "Please tell me you finished bringing in the bags."

Janice crossed her arms over her chest. "Come down here."

"Why?"

"The police would like to ask a few questions."

"Police?"

Sabrina stepped out of the bedroom with her phone in her hand. "I'm going to call Antonio."

Shit. "Call Turin first."

The police coming to my house could only spell trouble. The officer's nasally voice made me cringe as I got closer. "I'm Gigi Bresciani."

The officer lifted his badge in front of my face. "Detective Soren, and this is Raymond."

I placed a hand on my stomach. "Yes, detectives. How can I help you?"

"Do you know Igor Mendoza?"

Sabrina snapped. "Don't answer that."

I raised an eyebrow. "Why are you at my home?"

"We have a few questions about the death of Igor Mendoza."

"Not sure how I can help you."

Detective Soren glanced around my home. "Nothing to be alarmed about unless you're hiding something."

Someone had betrayed me if the detectives were at my home investigating Igor's death.

"Do you know Hugo Mendoza?"

"I'd suggest you speak with my attorney for further questions—" My words were cut short as I bent over in pain. "Oh god."

"Gigi! Are you all right?" Sabrina rushed to my side, coaching me to take deep breaths. "I think the baby is coming."

"I'll have to ask you to leave," Janice told the detectives firmly.

Sabrina helped me to stand. "Hold on, Gigi. Janice, go grab her baby bag."

I watched the detectives stroll to their vehicle. "Take

their license plate," I said as Sabrina helped me into the passenger seat.

Ralfie started the car as Janice jogged out of the house and slipped into the backseat with my bags.

I rubbed my stomach and continued to take deep breaths. "Ugh! The pain," I grumbled, wondering if I really could be a good mom.

* * *

Present

I smiled at my son as he cooed in Sabrina's arms.

"Are you going to tell him about the police coming by the house?" Janice asked.

Axel had checked himself out of the hospital a few hours ago, but I had one more day before we could be home together. Giving birth to my son had been the most beautiful thing in the world, and also the most painful, which had me rethinking a large family.

"Axel will want to kill them," I replied.

"Maybe he should," Janice mumbled under her breath.

Sabrina pinned her eyes on Janice. "Not funny, Janice."

"What happened with Igor Mendoza?" Sabrina laid my baby boy down.

"Nothing happened that shouldn't have."

"Should we get Carlo and Antonio to help?" Janice looked concerned.

"No, I need to handle some stuff on my own."

Janice reminded me, "Axel is going to want answers."

"When that time comes, I'll answer them. But for now, I want to enjoy my son."

I got out of bed and Sabrina helped me to the bathroom to wash up. I felt sick to my stomach, worrying about the blowback from Igor's death. It reminded me to check with Turin to find out how it got out. After I brushed my hair, washed my face, and changed my gown, I crawled back into bed.

"We're going to head home to our babies. Keep us updated on what you need," Janice said.

"I'll be fine," I said as I hugged the two women.

Sabrina gave me a final squeeze. "We'll be here tomorrow to help you leave."

The girls checked on my son one more time and waved goodbye.

I picked up my phone and saw a message from Axel.

Axel: *I made it home. Are you and my son okay?*

Me: *Yes, he's sleeping right now.*

Axel: *Turin will be there tomorrow to bring you home.*

Me: *Don't worry about me. Sabrina and Janice will bring me home.*

Axel: *We need to discuss some changes when you get here.*

I chose not to respond to that. Axel would do anything to protect our family, but he reminded me of Dario in some ways when it came to my being in the cartel. The culture of the cartel was that women stayed out of the men's business and tended to the home.

I logged out of the thread and went to Turin's message thread.

Me: *Call me asap.*

* * *

Finally, after two days in the hospital, I was on my way home with our son. Axel was waiting for me there with the nurse we'd hired to take care of him. Turin was busy, and I needed to schedule a meeting to discuss Igor and Hugo. The car pulled up in front of the house and Ralfie approached the passenger door to grab my bags. I steadied myself and let him pick up the car seat. Sabrina stood next to me as I slowly walked into the house.

I released a breath as I took in the peace and quiet. "Where's Axel?"

Janice took the car seat from Ralfie. "In the bedroom with the nurse."

"I'm going to check on him and then feed the baby."

I heard low voices outside the door and pushed it open to see the nurse with Axel. "How is he doing?"

"Stubborn, but fine," the nurse answered.

Axel flinched as she checked his blood pressure.

"Are you in pain?" I moved toward him and leaned in to look him in the eye.

"I'll be fine." He grabbed the back of my head and kissed me on the lips.

I wiped the lipstick from his mouth. "You're lying."

His nurse removed the stethoscope and stepped out of the room.

"Where's my son?" Axel asked.

"Janice has him." I sat on the bed.

Axel extended his palm to my stomach. "Can't believe I missed your pregnancy."

"You'll make new memories." Our hands interlocked.

Axel rested his head on the headboard. "Not the same. Dario took you away from me."

"Dario will answer for that." My heart skittered when his hand went to my thigh. I craved every inch of him.

"Not soon enough."

I trailed my fingers along his cheek. "The only thing you need to focus on is your health, Axel."

He closed his eyes. "Turin filled me in on a few details."

"All of that can be discussed later."

"Avoiding it won't help."

I frowned. "Who says I'm avoiding anything?"

"I know the truth, Gigi."

My mind stilled at the thought of him being angry with me about killing Igor. I tried to climb off the bed. "Axel," I complained as he grabbed my arm and pulled me down on top of him. "You'll hurt yourself. I'm too heavy."

His hands moved to my butt and down to my thighs. "Turin told me that Rosa, Lamberto, and Edmundo all worked together to plan my parents' death and frame Laurent."

"Yes," I whispered. Rosa had resented me for being headstrong and wanting a different life than the one she'd planned. But to kill innocent people to get her way? That was cold.

Axel looked me in the eye. "I want you to step down."

I tried to move, and he tightened his grip. "Let me go." I pushed my hand flat on his chest.

"Gigi, let me explain." His face was hard, his voice commanding.

"Not right now. I need to feed the baby."

His eyes searched my face. "He's fine."

"Axel, I'm not talking about this right now."

He drew me closer, and his breath stirred my hair. "Dario will be found and killed."

"I know he will because I'm going to be the one to

do it."

He brushed his hand down my arm as I stood. "I feel like you're keeping something from me."

I looked over my shoulder at him as I strolled to the door. "Turin should keep his opinions about my business to himself."

"Gigi—"

"I'll have Ebony bring you something to eat."

"Gigi!" Axel yelled.

I wanted to tell him the truth but now wasn't the time with him still in pain. He was in a different headspace right now, and I didn't need judgment from my husband about how I handled people.

Janice passed me a plate of food. I sat next to Gaspare and smiled as I tugged on his tiny foot.

I had the house reconstructed after the bombing. Some people said I should have moved, but my father bought this place for me to start fresh.

"You seem pissed." Janice sat down next to me and grabbed a glass of iced tea.

I smiled at my son as I pushed the food around on my plate. "Ebony, can you send food up to my husband, please?"

"Yes, Mrs. Bresciani." Ebony reached for a tray and set up a plate for Axel.

I waited for her to finish and leave the kitchen to talk. "Axel wants me to step down."

Janice sighed. "You can't be surprised."

"Sabrina?" I wanted her opinion.

"He's seen a lot before you and knows how ugly it can get."

"Everybody acts like I'm some delicate flower. I know what I'm doing."

Janice tapped me on the shoulder. "We're on your side."

Gaspare started to cry, so I reached over to pick him up, unhooking my nursing bra to feed him. That put him in a better mood, and I patted his butt and rubbed his back.

Janice picked up her wineglass. "Only advice we can give you is to trust your husband. Dario will win if you shut Axel out."

"I'll tell him when the time is right," I said as Gaspare finished eating. I leaned him against my shoulder and burped him before putting him back in his seat to rest. "Did Axel eat?" I asked Ebony as she returned.

Ebony chuckled. "He said to make him a steak, rice, and potatoes."

I rolled my eyes. Axel had to go against the doctor's orders of eating healthy and building strength. "Thanks, Ebony."

I wiped Gaspare's face and finished my food while the girls continued to talk.

* * *

Later that night, I stood beneath the shower in our bathroom and let the hot water soothe my aches. I looked down at my stomach—it felt empty since the birth of my baby. Gaspare had experienced every emotion these past few months as I tried to keep him safe, and it was odd to be so alone in my body again.

I jumped as the shower door opened and strong arms wrapped around my waist. Axel kissed the back of my neck, and I leaned my head on his shoulder. "You shouldn't be out of bed."

"I'm sorry." He cupped my chin.

I traced his mouth with my fingertips. "For what?"

"Making you think I'm like Dario or your mother by trying to control you."

His thick, long girth pressed against my ass as he wrapped a hand around my neck. He turned my face, and his mouth locked in on mine.

Axel wasn't remotely similar to Dario. His hand slid down to my ass and I pulled back before things got out of control. "We can't. Not yet."

"I know. How long do we have to wait?"

"Six weeks." I grinned as he scowled.

Stepping out of his hold, I picked up the soapy sponge and turned to wash his chest.

Axel cupped my breast. "How the hell am I going to last six weeks?"

"You have no choice."

He grunted, kissed me again, and walked me back to the wall. Out of habit, I raised my leg around his hip and felt him growing hard. "Time to shower," I reminded him.

Axel bent to suckle my nipple and my heartbeat went crazy.

"Baby, you need to rest." I drew a shaky breath.

"I'll rest when I'm dead."

I laughed as he stepped back and finished washing. Stepping out of the shower, he picked up a large towel and dried off before leaving the bathroom. I washed and dried my hair and entered the bedroom to find Gaspare in bed with Axel.

"You didn't look like the type to bring a baby into the bedroom." I removed the towel and picked up my nightgown.

"I don't want you to wear that. I want you naked."

"Not in the mood to be naked."

Axel rose from the bed and placed Gaspare in the bassinet. He came around the bed and took my hand, pulling me in front of the mirror. A smile played on his lips. "You're beautiful."

I shook my head. "I just had a baby."

"You had *my* baby." He spoke softly.

"I don't feel beautiful." My hormones were all over the place.

"You're beautiful in here, and that's what matters," he said, touching my chest over my heart.

"Tomorrow, will you please follow the nurse's orders?"

"No." Axel moved away and climbed back into bed.

I joined him, pulling the covers over us and laying my head on his chest. "I want you to be healthy."

"I'm healthy. The doctor and nurses can work on me here at the house."

I caressed the side of his stomach. "But Axel, you just got out of a coma."

He sighed and turned off the bedroom lamp. "Go to sleep."

This conversation wasn't over. I planned to keep my eye on him and ensure he took his health seriously. Gaspare needed his dad in top shape. Maybe we could work out together; a routine to build Axel's strength and one for me to recover from childbirth.

Axel's light snores lingered in my ears as I watched him sleep. A smile curved my lips at having him back. There were so many things I wanted to tell him that he'd missed.

Chapter 5

Axel

The bedroom door squeaked open, startling me from sleep. I reached out to the empty spot where Gigi slept. I looked for the bassinet Gaspare had slept in last night, which was also gone.

"Mr. Bresciani, it's time to check your blood pressure," the nurse spoke softly as she entered.

"Where's my wife?"

"Mrs. Bresciani said she had a meeting and would check in with you later."

"Heather, right?"

"Yes."

"Just take my pressure and leave."

Heather put her bag on the floor. "Doctor Nathaniel said you shouldn't move around too much yet."

I turned my head away and ignored her comment.

Fifteen minutes later, I got up to shower and eat breakfast. Pissed that Gigi left without saying something, I grabbed my cell phone and dialed her number.

"She's pissing me off," I grumbled to myself.

The call went to voicemail. "Gigi, call me back, or I'm

coming to find you!" I growled as there was a knock at the front door. I strode to answer it. "Where is she?" I asked, opening the door to Turin.

Turin pushed his phone in front of my face, showing me a picture of Hugo Mendoza and one of Casella's men. "Gigi's called the guys for an early meeting about a new order increase with the Irish."

"Is that what she told you?" I demanded as we walked through the house to my office.

"After Alvar Casella's death, his people contacted Hugo Mendoza."

"About?"

"They want protection and a new partnership," he said with a somber expression.

"You're keeping something from me."

"Gigi killed Igor Mendoza."

I paused at the office door and whirled to face him. Turin knew how I felt about being kept out of the loop. "What the fuck do you mean, she killed him?"

We entered the office, and Turin went to my computer. He slid in a flash drive and opened it to a video of Gigi in a hotel.

I sat in the chair and watched Igor step off an elevator and slip into her hotel room. My fists clenched. "When were you going to tell me?"

"I got all the footage from the hotel, but Gigi's been on another level with making decisions," he confessed.

"How did you let her-"

"Fuck you, Axel," he cut across me angrily. "You're my brother, but she's the Boss."

"You should have put a stop to her even being in the same room as Igor."

"We can't change that now, and we have bigger problems."

"Hugo Mendoza," I stated.

"Hugo wants more territory and revenge for Igor."

"By working with Dario."

Turin leaned over my desk and pointed to pictures of Dario and Hugo together. "We know he took a flight from Mendoza's people. I think Dario put the plan together for them after Casella's death."

"Gigi's going to give up her position. I'm done." I announced.

Turin folded his arms. "She won't take it that easy."

"Gigi needs to listen."

"Hugo doesn't negotiate."

That would only give me more reason to kill him. "Hugo can go to hell."

I watched the video over and over, bombarding Turin with questions. Then I went to change clothes. It was time to make my presence known at the office.

* * *

Turin thought it would be a bad idea to interrupt, but Gigi and I didn't keep secrets from each other. I walked into the conference room as she was talking.

"I want the price to increase for Chicago, Philadelphia, and New York." Gigi stood in front of a few cartel men, giving directions.

"What if they don't take to the price increase?" one man probed.

Gigi insisted. "Make them understand."

"Give us a minute," I interjected, walking toward Gigi.

"Axel, what are you doing here?" Gigi looked startled.

"I could ask you the same question. My son is at home with the nanny."

Turin cleared his throat. "Give them a second, gentleman."

He opened the door for them to leave and followed them out.

Gigi moved toward me in a figure-hugging dress that was too short to be wearing in front of her men. "Why did you come here?"

"You killed Igor Mendoza," I stated, wrapping a hand around her wrist.

Gigi tried to move in close and kiss me, but I turned my head.

"Igor was working with Dario," she justified.

"I'm back now, and you will no longer be making decisions without me."

"It doesn't work like that, Axel."

"Laurent put those kinds of decisions in my hand as the Enforcer of the family."

"Laurent is no longer in charge."

"The decisions you're making will not end well if you don't include me as the Enforcer."

"I love you, but I know what I'm doing," she said calmly.

"You only got in this position because your father was killed, and I married you." I wanted to call my words back as soon as they came out of my mouth.

Silence fell and Gigi went rigid, her eyes flashing with pain.

"Gigi, I'm sorry—"

"No, it's fine."

I pressed close to the warmth of her body. "Baby, I didn't mean it."

"Do whatever you want to do, Axel. I'll go home and be a mother to our son." Gigi turned, snatched up her purse and left the boardroom.

"Fuck!" I slumped forward and rested my head in my hands.

Turin came back into the room. "Where is she going?"

"I said she got in this role because I married her."

Turin winced. "Damn, Axel."

"Get me Hugo's number."

"Should you be on your feet?"

"I have no choice."

"Something else I need to tell you."

"Turin, you're pissing me off."

"I heard the Irish want to move in fast. We need to let Antonio and Carlo know. If the Casellas and Mendozas come together, we're going to have even bigger problems."

"How much do the Irish want?" I inquired.

He shut the office door behind me as we left. "Enough that we'll need to agree or get rid of them before they join forces with Dario."

"I need more eyes on Dario. How the hell is he walking around free?" I demanded.

Turin and I walked off the elevator and out of the building.

"Watch it!" A guy yelled as he bumped into my shoulder.

I glared at him, feeling uneasy without my gun.

I climbed into the car and slammed the door,

watching the man stop to talk to another guy on the corner.

Turin started the car and merged with the traffic. Suddenly, he yanked the wheel sharply, narrowly avoiding the vehicle that had tried to sideswipe us.

"You good?" Turin shouted.

I nodded. "Get us out of here!"

Turin put the car in drive again. "Trying. These folks are crazy, not paying attention to lights."

My head swiveled left to right. "Fuck, come on." I was agitated after the near miss.

"Chill," Turin pumped the gas and moved into the middle lane. "What's gotten into you?"

"This shit has me paranoid."

"Hugo or Dario?"

I pulled out my phone and dialed Gigi's number. "Both."

"We need to get to the warehouse with the team."

"Gigi's not answering her phone."

"Give her time. You pissed her off."

Turin passed through boarded sections of Hoboken. I remembered we had a few spots holding our products close to the shipyard. Turin parked the car, and we strolled to the door. I leaned against the doorframe for a second to catch my breath.

Turin frowned. "Are you sure you're up to this meeting?"

"Yeah, I'll be fine."

"We can wait until you're fully back."

My gaze flicked to my best friend. "I can handle myself."

"Keep your attitude with Gigi, not me," Turin said, pushing the door open.

The place had electricity and an assembly line of products running in and out. Nothing like our farm in Italy but big enough to stay off the grid.

"Boss, glad to see you back." Miguel held a hand out for me to shake.

Turin folded his arms. "Miguel, what are we looking like?"

Miguel didn't show fear, and I appreciated a man who wasn't easily intimidated.

"Turin and Gigi demanded we do three ships a week. I manage all the locations, and so far, we've had no issues."

"Nothing unusual?" I challenged.

Miguel pondered my question. "A few times, I thought we may have been followed, but I couldn't be sure."

Turin's eyes narrowed as he searched Miguel's face. "You never told me."

Miguel shrugged. "I didn't think anything of it until now." He moved closer and his voice dropped low. "At the last drop off, they took the product and didn't wait for us to count the money."

My eyes narrowed on Miguel. "How many times has this happened?"

"At least twice." Miguel took his phone out to show his last few drops.

"Who was the buyer?" My head was spinning.

"Irish boys," Miguel answered, putting his phone back in his pocket.

Turin and I looked at each other. One time could be forgiven, but multiple times made me question if Dario had set this up from the beginning.

"I need names—"

I was cut off as the warehouse plunged into darkness. I had no weapon, and Turin shoved me behind him as gunfire erupted.

"We need to get to the cars!" Turin barked.

I crawled to the wall as bullets sprayed through the windows, taking down a few of our men, including Miguel.

Turin's expression was grim. "Stay close to me."

Tires squealed from the back, and Turin gestured toward the side doors he'd had installed for emergencies. The doors opened to a tunnel that led us out to the woods. I was winded from running, which only increased my frustration and anger. Sweat dripped down my face. I followed Turin, who aimed his gun high in front of us.

I removed my phone from my pocket. "We need to keep moving to get a phone signal."

Turin jerked his head in a nod. "That was a setup."

"Too easy," I mumbled.

I was livid. What if Gigi had come with us tonight? The thought of my wife being in danger made my blood burn.

We emerged from the woods and headed for a nearby gas station. Turin made a few calls while I dialed Gigi's number.

"Axel, it's late," Gigi said groggily.

"Listen to me, Gigi," I said urgently.

"What's wrong?" she asked breathlessly.

"We were ambushed," I said as Turin finished his call. I glanced back at the woods and warehouse beyond.

"Where are you?"

A car arrived, and Turin motioned for me to get in.

"On my way back to you."

"Tell me what happened, Axel."

"Someone thought we would be easy targets and tried to put a hit on us."

The urge to kill whoever was responsible was bubbling to the surface, ready to blow for threatening my family and me.

"Are you with Turin?"

"Yes. We'll be there in thirty minutes."

"Get here safe." Gigi's concern soothed my frazzled nerves.

"I will." I disconnected the call.

We were overzealous tonight and put ourselves in a vulnerable situation. The setup had Dario's stamp all over it.

All the lights were off in the house when we arrived. I ran inside and made a beeline for Gaspare's room. He was sound asleep in his crib. I pulled his cover over his little body and kissed his forehead lightly.

Slipping quietly from his room, I headed for the bedroom and saw Gigi still awake, reading a book.

"Thank God you're back. Are you okay?" she asked when she saw me, dropping her book on the bedside table.

"I'm fine, baby." I kissed her on the forehead and kicked off my shoes.

"Do you want to talk about it?"

I shook my head. "Tomorrow. For now, I just want to wash off the day and hold my wife."

If there was one thing Gigi understood, it was that sometimes you had to leave the stress at "work."

Grabbing a quick shower, I pulled on clean boxers and crawled into bed. I drew Gigi close to my chest and kissed the back of her neck. Calmed by her presence, I succumbed to sleep.

* * *

Sunlight filtered into the room, and I opened my eyes to see Gigi gazing at me. I used to wake alone, usually after carrying out a job for Laurent, but now I had a wife and child. I was a lucky fucker.

Gaspare whimpered in the room next to us, and Gigi kissed my chest before going to get him. She brought him in and sat on the loveseat in the window. Tension from our conversation in the office yesterday lingered in the air, but Gigi smiled at me.

I stretched and threw the covers back, moving to Gigi and dropping to my knees in front of her.

Gigi grinned at me. "You snored last night."

I chuckled. "I was tired."

"Must have been all that running away from bullets." Gigi grabbed my hand and intertwined our fingers. "Are you hungry?"

"Maybe later."

I stood and looked down at our son before moving to open the window. Gigi placed Gaspare in his bassinet and wrapped her arms around me from behind. The birds chirped, and the wind tossed the leaves around. Summer was coming. Soon we would be out in the pool and using the guest house.

"When I was pregnant, I craved pickles and yogurt."

I wrinkled my nose in disgust. "That's gross."

Gigi laughed. "Plus gas and the way your son sat on my bladder. I felt like he knew you weren't around."

She turned to lean against the window so she was facing me. I moved closer and braced my hands on either side of her.

"I'm here now. Do you still crave pickles with

yogurt?" I would have the chef throw it away not to tempt her again.

She burst into laughter. "No."

"Good."

"Pregnancy cravings are normal."

"Yeah, but I didn't get to have you bugging me to pick something up in the middle of the night or rub your swollen feet." I pointed at her feet, and we both laughed. Moments like this felt like old times.

Gaspare fussed, and Gigi moved away to pick him up. "I don't like how we acted yesterday," she said as she sat on the edge of the bed with our son.

"I've never doubted your strength, but when it comes to Dario, I need you to step back."

"Explain last night." She rubbed Gaspare's back.

"Turin and I went to check on the product. He had a few close contacts with a Russian deal that might hurt us if they work with Hugo Mendoza."

"Hugo wants revenge for Igor."

"Yes, and I need my wife to stay out of harm's way."

"Too late if he knows I killed his nephew."

"He knows."

Gigi bounced Gaspare on her lap. "For now, I'll cut back on my duties."

"No, I need you to step down. It's time."

"How can you ask me to go against what my father wanted?"

"Laurent wanted you safe, and Dario would've been in charge if you'd married him."

"So my mother gets her wish," she said, her voice heavy with sarcasm.

Gaspare let out a wail of hunger and she lifted her shirt, helping him to latch on.

I frowned. "Gigi, this has nothing to do with your mother."

Gigi said nothing as she nursed Gaspare. After a few minutes, he was finished, and I took him from her to burp him.

"Okay." Gigi finally responded as she fixed her shirt.

I tossed the covers back and placed our son further up on the bed near the pillows. I cupped Gigi's chin and tilted her face to look at me. "You and our son are my world. I'll move heaven and earth to keep you safe."

She wrapped hers around my neck. "I believe you."

I dropped a kiss on the tip of her nose. "Then trust me."

"I hate this. It feels like he's winning," she said unhappily.

I placed my hand over her heart. "Dario will feel the full force of my wrath."

Gigi needed to recover after giving birth, and I needed to recover from my ordeal. Dario had screwed over so many people, I half hoped he would end up dead without me even touching him. Hugo had chosen to work with the Devil.

I stared into her eyes and smiled. "How are you feeling?"

"Tired, but good."

"Did Gaspare sleep through the night?"

We glanced at him trying to fall asleep on the bed.

Gigi smiled. "He's a light sleeper, like his father."

"I want to take you both out for lunch."

"Are you sure? With everything that happened last night?"

"More guards will be assigned to you."

Gigi groaned and stood. "Axel, that's exhausting."

"For your safety and my peace of mind."

She sighed. "Okay." She walked to the closet and looked through her clothes.

My phone rang, and I grabbed it from the bedside table. "Axel."

"I wondered if you'd have the guts to pick up the phone."

"Who is this?"

"Hugo Mendoza."

"How did you get my number?" I demanded.

"Meet me in one hour."

Gigi stepped out of the closet with two dresses.

"No one summons me to a meeting. I do the calling."

Mendoza chuckled, and I balled my hand into a fist. Gigi moved to stand in front of me.

"My people will call you when I'm ready to meet," I countered.

"Your wife killed my godson," he sneered.

"Being on the wrong side of this fight to save Dario won't end well for you."

"My loyalty to the Ramini family is for life," Hugo answered.

"He's being funded by you, correct?"

Hugo chuckled again. "One hour."

The line went dead.

Gigi looked at me expectantly.

"There's something I need to take care of, baby."

"Do what needs to be done, Axel. I won't question you."

Her passive-aggressive attitude pissed me off. I didn't like being an asshole, so I let her leave the room while I contacted Turin to pick me up. A day with Gigi and my son was my priority after I discovered Hugo's intentions.

Once dressed, I got Gigi and our son settled in the limo. I kissed his head and Gigi's cheek before telling Ralfie that two cars would tail them.

"There's no need to worry," Gigi said as she shut the door.

I leaned down and spoke through the open window. "You've got two SVUs with guards following you as a precaution." I pointed behind at the two cars of soldiers ready to die for our family.

"Be safe," Gigi said.

"Make sure your phone is on," I replied and got in the car to head out first.

Chapter 6

Gigi

A few days later.

Axel and I avoided talking about Hugo. The dominant Enforcer in him was slowly seeping back into my life. Tonight, I wanted to go out and enjoy myself after the birth of my son. I was a cartel Boss and a mother, but this evening was about being Gigi. Janice had mentioned a new club called Sinful. It was in the middle of New York's Times Square with two levels, glass ceilings, neon lights, and a large dance floor. The VIP areas had one-way mirrors for privacy.

Janice waved her hands in the air as she danced. Some people would scoff at us being friends since I was so much younger, but I appreciated her and Sabrina as women in their early forties giving me wisdom about being married and being a mom in the mob.

Our bottle girl came to the table with our drinks. I slipped her two hundred dollars to keep the drinks coming, and she smiled. I pushed to my feet, grabbed my vodka and soda, and watched my girls enjoy their night out.

"We're here now, so give it up." Janice urged me to talk.

"What should I give up?" I questioned.

Janice and Sabrina laughed. Tonight was meant to be fun with no talk about our husbands.

"Lie about being pissed at Axel." Sabrina snapped her fingers, bobbing her head to the music. One of Janice's girlfriends stood, strolled down the stairs, talked to the guard, and then laughed.

"Not pissed at him." Sabrina said. "We've seen and done it all with our men, even tried to make them jealous."

Janice said, "Nothing can get past them."

"When Axel found out I'd done something that could harm us, he was upset."

"Something like what?"

"Have you ever put yourselves in harm's way by taking matters into your own hands?"

"All the time in the beginning." Janice bent forward and picked up her glass. She pushed my drink into my hand, and I gulped it down.

"He hates me because I made him marry me." My eyes raked over the crowd.

"You didn't make him marry you." Janice moved to the beat of the music.

I pressed a hand to my stomach. "Can we not talk and just enjoy the music?"

"We can, but you must come to terms with your brand-new life." Janice took the glass out of my hand and refilled it.

"My father wanted me to be strong, but I feel foolish and weak."

Sabrina touched my shoulder and smiled. "Gigi, you're still learning."

The sweat rolled off my forehead. "I feel like an idiot sometimes."

"Join the mommy club." Sabrina continued. She nudged my arm with her shoulder and gestured to the dance floor.

"As a Boss, I felt in control and powerful, like nothing could touch me." I met Sabrina's eyes.

"You craved power, and now you're a mom, you're trying to convince yourself you can have it all." Janice said, holding my gaze.

"Yes! My father handled business and took good care of me." I slammed the glass on the table and poked my lip out.

"If you think about it, was your father around for all the moments?" Sabrina asked.

I evaded her question and plastered a smile on my face, raising my glass in a toast.

"Tonight, you must shed it all, get out, and have fun," Janice stated.

We clicked glasses and drained the rest of our drinks. Janice took me by the hand and marched down the stairs into the crowd, with JayZ playing in the background. It might come as a surprise to some people, but he was extremely popular in Italy. Sabrina joined us, her guard keeping space between us and the crowd. I clapped as she whirled in a circle with her hands in the air and the rest of the girls joined us on the floor. It was refreshing to be carefree again.

* * *

Thirty minutes later, I was tired, hot, and sweaty. I was ready to see my baby and head to bed. Janice walked back to the section where we'd ordered. Sabrina grabbed my hand, and I followed her through the crowd. I was watching the other women flirting with single guys when I caught something in my peripheral vision.

"Ginerva?" I whispered.

I bumped into Sabrina as she suddenly stopped behind her guard. "Shit! Sorry," I apologized.

Sabrina put her hand on my arm. "My bad."

"I think I've had too much to drink." I blinked, wondering if I was imagining things.

"Why do you say that?" Sabrina followed my gaze.

I pointed at the couple in the corner near the edge of the bar. The guy's back was to us, but the woman looked like my old friend.

"Ginerva!" I yelled, but she didn't turn.

Janice came back down the stairs. "Time to go, ladies."

"Wait! I need to see something." I yanked my hand out of Sabrina's grip and darted through the crowd. My bodyguards would be pissed that I'd run off.

I was a short distance away when a man blocked my path. "What's your hurry, sexy?"

"Excuse me." I tried to pass him.

He stepped in front of me again. "Come on. You look like you need me in your life."

Usually I would have been happy to put him in his place, but I had bigger priorities right now. "Leave, or prepare to be questioned by my two friends," I warned, indicating my approaching bodyguards.

He smirked. "They can come with us. There's a lot of me to handle." He grabbed his crotch.

I snapped my finger, and Michael, one of the new guards, clapped his hand on the guy's shoulder. He turned him around and escorted him away. When I looked back at the corner, it was empty.

I strode closer and tapped my hand on the counter of the bar. "Hey!" I waved to grab the bartender's attention.

"What will it be?"

"Did you see where that couple went that was standing here?"

His brow rose high. "Couple?"

"The girl and guy all hugged up."

Bartender replied, "Sorry, I don't know what you're talking about."

"They were here for a few minutes making out," I countered.

The vibration of the music increased, and the crowd started screaming. It was hard to hear him.

A hand tapped on the bar top. "Mrs. Bresciani."

I looked up in surprise. "Detective Soren. You don't seem like a hookah bar type."

"Interesting to see you here tonight."

"I need to get back to my friends." I walked around him, but he grabbed my hand.

"Do you?"

"Detective, you need to let go of my hand."

"What's the hurry?" he questioned, though he released my hand.

I looked over his shoulder to see Janice heading toward me, followed by our guards.

"Are you following me, detective?" I challenged.

"I wasn't expecting to see you here." He rested his hands at his side.

"I bet."

"Gigi, time to go," Janice interrupted.

Axel could clear this place in seconds if I asked, but I wanted to have fun. "Not ready to leave."

"Axel called Carlo. He said you need to call him now." Janice held her phone up and wiggled it in front of my face.

Detective Soren smirked like he knew something.

"Detective, you might fool some people, but not me. If I find out you're following my friends and me, I'll have my lawyer sue you."

"Mrs. Bresciani, if you change your mind, give me a call." He pulled a business card out of his pocket and held it up for me to take.

I ignored his offer and walked outside to our awaiting limo, still searching the area for that familiar woman. Janice climbed in next to Sabrina, and I slid in behind her.

Sabrina looked out of the window. "He's going to be trouble."

"Who?" I questioned.

She gestured out the window.

Detective Soren stood near the alley of the club, watching intently as our limo drove away.

I took a napkin out of my purse to wipe the sweat off my face. "I think I saw Ginerva tonight."

Janice took out her makeup case and touched up. "Your best friend, Ginerva, who was kidnapped?"

I fanned myself. "I know it sounds crazy."

"When?" Janice asked.

"Walking back to the VIP section."

"How did she get here?" Sabrina had the same thoughts as me.

I grabbed a bottle of water from the small fridge to cool down. "There's no way she's in America. I mean, we've tried everything to find her, and prayed Dario didn't kill her." I sighed and turned the air on in the car.

"Stranger things have happened," Janice muttered.

* * *

I passed Gaspare to the doctor at his follow-up visit the next day. Axel wasn't happy about me going out to the club last night. I'd told him we were having a girls' night in at Janice's.

The doctor was curious. "Gaspare looks happy and healthy. Is he sleeping through the night?"

"He wakes a few times, but for the most part, he sleeps until the morning."

"And you are breastfeeding, correct?"

I touched Gaspare's cheek. "Not the best feeling in the world, but he's latching on fine."

"Great. I like to hear that. What about you?"

"Do you think she should drink while breastfeeding?" Axel asked.

I tensed in shock. "Axel!"

"It's fine, Gigi. He can ask me anything he wants."

Emotion contracted my throat. "He's being rude."

"As long as she's taking precautions, pumping beforehand and waiting afterward, a little wine won't hurt."

"I went out the other night, Doctor, and he's pissed." I waved Axel off.

"You two have to trust each other. Gaspare can pick up on any hostility." She finished documenting his information.

I put him in his car seat, and Axel picked it up to leave the room. The doctor explained to bring him back in a few weeks for a follow up, so we made the appointment and went to the car.

"Ralfie's taking you home," Axel announced.

I noticed another car in front of my limo with our guards. "Where are you going?"

He swung around to face me. "I have business."

"So that's how we're acting, Axel?" I challenged, my frustration bubbling up.

"Gigi, you're pushing my buttons."

"I go out one time—"

"It's not just about going out." His face darkened. "Anything could have happened. I thought you were at Janice's house."

"We have triple the protection now."

He stared deeply into my eyes as he framed my face with his hands. "Dario is still out there."

I slipped my hands around his waist. "I know."

"Then act like it!" he growled.

Gaspare started to cry, and tears stung my eyes. I pulled away from him. "Take me home."

"Baby, listen." He tipped my face toward his.

My fight to make my voice heard was an issue from the past. Axel wasn't Rosa or my father. Letting my guard down with my husband showed I was open to his feelings.

"I'm afraid I'll end up like my parents," I confessed as I reached out to soothe Gaspare in his car seat.

"We're not your parents or mine," Axel reminded me.

As Gaspare cooed, I picked up the bottle I had in the fridge from pumping and placed it in his mouth. "I'm sorry about last night." I whispered, suddenly aware of what the outcome could have been.

"We need to put everything on the line." Axel

scanned my face as he slipped into the car. He'd obviously decided to ride with us.

Ralfie started the car and drove out of the parking lot. Axel nipped at my neck, then nuzzled his chin over my shoulder.

"I know you're mad about last night, but something else happened."

"What happened?"

"Detective Soren was there and tried to talk to me. The same detective who came to the house."

"Came to our house when?"

I took a deep breath and exhaled. "The day I gave birth to Gaspare. They came to our house to talk about Igor Mendoza."

Axel removed his arm from around my shoulder. "They pushed you into early labor," he muttered, his mouth hardening.

"I was already overdue."

"Things could have gone wrong," he bit out.

"He has a partner, Detective Raymond."

"What else do I need to know?"

"I think I saw Ginerva."

Ralfie arrived at our home, and Axel helped me out of the car. He took Gaspare and wrapped his other hand around my waist as we walked to the front door.

"I thought you had business to handle," I said, looking up at him.

"That can wait. I want to make sure we're good." Axel smiled and kissed my cheek.

"We're always good." I cupped his face and smoothed my thumb over his beard.

I removed my jacket as Axel took Gaspare to his play pen in the living room. I could hear Ebony and Heather in the kitchen as I followed Axel to his office and closed the door.

"Dario kidnapped Ginerva," I said, picking up the conversation now we were alone. He sat at his desk and turned his computer on. "I remember."

I paced the room. "We never saw a body."

Axel rubbed his temples. "We know Igor Mendoza helped Dario to get to America through Igor's uncle Hugo."

I sat on the edge of the desk. "Then Soren and Raymond came asking questions."

Axel leaned back in his chair in thought. "Plus, the ambush at the warehouse."

An idea flickered in my mind. "You think they're connected?"

With a sour look, Axel remarked. "Yes."

I sighed. "Dario's a skilled manipulator."

"Dario is out of control."

"I want to find Ginerva."

"Ask Turin to pull the footage from the cameras at the club."

I stood to leave. "Thank you."

"Gigi?"

I turned to look at him. "Yes?"

"Never keep anything from me."

"I had my reasons."

"Doesn't matter the reasons. It could have been avoided."

"You were in a coma, Axel. I wanted you to recover." I reached the door and turned the knob to leave. "Going back and forth with you is like hitting my head against a brick wall."

"No more clubs, Gigi."

I stomped up the stairs to the bedroom, shutting the door and leaning against it. Ginerva was alive. I could feel it in my bones. If she had escaped, Dario would be looking for her. I needed to find and protect her. Bringing her here under our watch was the best thing we could do for her. Axel and I didn't agree on everything, but I knew my safety was his priority. His request for me not to get involved in cartel business was out of the question while our enemies were joining forces.

I picked up the phone to dial Sabrina's number, sitting near the window and listening to the phone ring.

"Hey, Gigi. How did Gaspare do at the doctor's office?" she questioned immediately.

The question put a smile on my face. "He's doing good."

"Everything okay?"

"I need your help."

She probed further. "With what?"

"I want to find Ginerva."

"I thought Axel said to stay out of everything."

"Axel has enough to deal with."

Sabrina responded, "Maybe you should let him handle finding her, Gigi."

"Sabrina, if it was Janice in trouble, you'd go to the ends of the earth to find her."

Sabrina was like a big sister, wanting to protect me. "Janice and I are different."

"No different to Ginerva and me."

"Let me call Janice on three-way."

"Thanks."

A minute passes before I hear kids laughing in the background. "Sabrina, you know Carlo went to handle some business, and I'm stuck babysitting."

"Girl, those are your kids."

"I only claim them for tax time," Janice said.

I wanted to laugh so badly, but Axel walked through the door.

"Gigi is on the line," Janice added.

Axel removed his shirt, dropped his pants, kicked off his boxers, and headed to the bathroom. I admired my husband's naked body. I missed being with him in that way. Six weeks seemed like forever, and I was desperate to be intimate with him.

"Gigi wants to do what?" Janice screeched, and I hurriedly ended the call. I jumped up and sauntered to the bathroom door, watching Axel bathe.

"You going to stay and watch me?" he teased.

"No, I need to check on Gaspare." I said quickly, coming up with an excuse.

There was a teasing smile on his face. "Come here, Gigi."

I whined. "Axel, I can't."

As he pushed his hand down his chest, he licked his lips. "Why?"

"I'm too emotional right now, and we might take it there before my time is up."

He threw his head back in a laugh.

"That's not funny!" I exclaimed.

The fire in his eyes blazed down at me. "I know how to shower without having sex with you."

"No..." I hesitated, torn between what I wanted and what I worried might happen if I gave in.

He slid the door open and held out a hand out for me. Our eyes locked. I kicked off my shoes and strolled to the door, removed my clothes before stepping inside. He turned to me and dragged his hand down my cheek. I closed my eyes and took in his presence. All those months I was without him, I'd pictured us together like this.

"We're meant to be," he assured me gently.

A rush of goosebumps spread over my body. "I missed you so much."

"Nothing will keep us apart."

There was a knot in my stomach. "Don't leave me again."

He gripped my throat lightly. "Never."

"How are you feeling?"

He pulled me in close, his fingers wrapped around my waist. "I'm fine," he responded dismissively.

"You're not a doctor, Axel."

Axel pushed his fingers through my hair and kissed me, slicking his tongue against mine.

I gripped his shoulders and moaned. My body was so sensitive to his touch. I wished we'd go to bed and make love all night long. But I was still recovering from giving birth, and it would be foolish to jump back into sex too soon.

Axel dropped to his knees, threw my right leg over his shoulder, and pressed his face into my pussy.

"Axel!" I yelped and tried to step back.

He locked his arms around my thighs and gripped my hips. I almost stumbled from the intensity of his touch and grabbed his shoulders to hold myself up. My heart jolted and my pulse pounded as the water cascaded over our bodies. Our attraction had been instant from the first time we met.

Axel kneaded my ass as he buried his face in between my thighs, and a familiar ripple of excitement washed over me. My mouth dropped open as he gently dragged his tongue from my pussy up to my stomach and circled around my navel. I moved to cover myself, but he stopped me and pressed a kiss to my skin.

"You know better than to hide yourself from me."

The passion in his eyes as he looked up at me invoked an urgency to please him. Axel brushed another kiss over my stomach and stood, kissing me deeply. Reaffirming our bond, I gripped his steel rod and squeezed.

"Shit, Gigi." he groaned.

"Never hide yourself from me, either."

"I won't, baby."

I slowly dropped a kiss on his chest, on each nipple, and down his stomach before taking him in my mouth. He gripped my head, and I watched him writhe under my control. We spent a pleasurable ten minutes in the shower before we dried off. Our makeup sessions always made up for the fights.

Chapter 7

Axel

Three days earlier.

Turin drove us to the hotel where Hugo stayed while he was in New York. The bar was cleared for us to meet, and I let him do most of the talking.

Hugo smiled at the server as she sashayed away from the table. "I would have respected your wife more if she'd come to me first."

"My wife doesn't answer to you."

Hugo's brows shot up. "Aren't you the Enforcer of the Carrington Cartel?"

"Are we discussing solutions, or feeding your ego?" I asked maliciously.

"Axel," Turin warned, keeping me calm.

His grin was snakelike. "I only talk to Bosses."

"You're talking to one."

"My nephew is dead, and we're owed compensation," Hugo explained.

"Not my problem."

"I believe there's evidence of her killing him," Hugo said casually.

Turin told me that someone at the hotel had sold a copy of the video, and that's how word got back to Hugo.

I shifted in my seat, frustrated that he had an upper hand. "I want Dario Ramini."

Hugo lifted a hand and picked up his sunglasses to place on his nose. "Dario is off limits."

"Then we have nothing else to discuss."

"I'll go with the Irish, and your wife will end up in jail."

I lunged at him. Turin held me back as Hugo's men pulled out their guns.

Hugo held up a hand to stay his men. "She owes me."

"Igor's replacement is worth a million, maybe two."

He glared. "Money won't make me feel better. I want territory."

"Not giving you all of Chicago."

"You'll give me Chicago and New York."

Hugo reached in his pocket, pulled out his phone. He played a video showing Gigi at the hotel.

"Any visitors to your home lately?" he asked snidely. "Detectives Soren and Raymond."

Knowing he was behind the cops coming to our place pissed me off even more. "Tell me, Hugo, are you planning to leave here alive?"

He chortled, grabbed his scotch, and drank it before answering. "I'm in New York for a few more days. Let me know what you want to do." Hugo slid out of the booth and buttoned his jacket before leaving with his men.

Present

Gigi slept like a baby last night, after I got back from the office. She told me all the time that she couldn't sleep well without me beside her in bed. I prayed God watched over my family because the decisions I was making were meant to protect them if I was no longer around.

Gigi held Gaspare in her arms in the backyard pool. I stood at the door watching while considering how I could get to Hugo and Dario before they made a move again.

Turin stepped beside me and passed me a drink. "Does she know?"

I turned to look at him, shaking my head. "Not yet."

"If we want to avoid further bloodshed, how should we handle it??"

My hand tightened around the glass. "As far as my wife and child are concerned, it is not possible."

"I found the hotel employee who gave Hugo the video."

"Any problems with the family?"

"Burial was tasteful."

Gaspare clung to Gigi as she floated in the water.

"I want to take her to Italy and keep them safe."

"She won't go for that easily."

"Killing another cartel Don will put us on the radar of the police and FBI."

"We have a few contacts. I can see how much Detective Soren and Raymond have on Gigi."

"I need everything from blood type to their mothers' birthdays."

"Look at it from Gigi's standpoint. She was pregnant and not thinking clearly."

"What did you find on Ginerva?"

"Nothing so far. I've been looking into Hugo's contacts and the shootout at the warehouse."

"Get more people on Ginerva. Gigi's losing her mind and feeling guilty."

Turin agreed. "We'll figure it out. Oh, and you won't

be surprised to know that Hugo was behind the shooting at the warehouse."

He was right. That news was no surprise to me.

Turin stared off into space as Gaspare splashed the water. He downed his drink quickly. "Killing won't be easy like Alvar Casella, Rosa, or Edmundo."

"It's time to come up with a new plan to deal with him since he wants all of Chicago and New York. We need another meeting."

Turin grunted, knowing how hotheaded I could be. "That won't be good for any of us."

Gigi stepped out of the pool and sauntered toward us with Gaspare. I picked up the towel, wrapped it around them, and kissed her forehead.

"Turin, what are you doing here?"

Turin tickled Gaspare's feet. "I needed to talk with Axel."

Gigi bounced Gaspare in her arms. "What about?"

"Hugo."

"Has he changed his mind about Igor and revealed Dario's location?" she asked.

"Hugo's not letting Igor's death go," I replied.

Gigi snapped. "Fuck Igor." She turned her attention to my best friend. "Turin, tell Axel I was right to kill Igor."

His shoulders slumped. "Gigi, I told you not to kill him."

Gigi glared at Turin.

"Hugo wants Chicago and New York or he'll send a video to the police," I explained.

"We have people on the force, but we can't pull them in without raising suspicions of Soren and Raymond," Turin added.

"I need to change Gaspare." Gigi walked back into the house.

Turin passed me another drink. "How are you feeling after the coma? For real?"

"Sometimes, I feel fine, and other times like shit. I'm still getting my body back in shape."

"Maybe you need to wait and rest a bit more before going on this mission to get Hugo and Dario."

"I'll rest when they're dead."

* * *

Gigi and I spent the day together after Turin left and let Gaspare hang with Janice and Sabrina's kids so they could meet finally. I promised the ladies Gigi would host something at the house when I felt it was safe.

Turin picked me up, and we had two of our guns in another vehicle a few cars down for backup. Turin turned the lights off in the car and I checked my weapons, nodding that I was ready.

Hugo was here with his people at dinner, and I wanted to wait to see if he contacted Dario when he left. I sat back in the seat and watched the front door of the restaurant intently as customers came and went.

"We only watch tonight," Turin cautioned.

"Unless they try something."

"I told Gigi I'd get you back in one piece." Turin and Gigi had become good friends while I was in the coma.

I stared intensely at the restaurant door, unable to place the man standing with his friends under the light. Something felt off. Then I realized it was the same guy who'd bumped into me a few weeks ago.

"I know him from the office."

Turin surveyed them from the window. "What?"

"The guy in the front."

"What guy? There are three of them."

"The one on the left in the black leather coat and gray slacks."

"At the office when?"

"The day we got side swiped and almost killed at the warehouse."

Turin's head swiveled around fast. "You're shitting me."

"What are the odds these men are here at the same restaurant as Hugo?"

"Extremely rare."

"They set us up." I reached to open the door.

Turin grabbed my hand before I could open it. "Yeah, but we can't do anything right now."

"I'm sending a message."

Turin gripped the steering wheel. "Too many people around."

"Wait until they get to their cars."

"Shit, Axel, we might need to rethink if Hugo comes out."

"He'll get the message that I'm willing to go anywhere and do anything to protect my wife."

"Gigi's a sister to me, but we'd be killing them without cause right now."

I cocked the chamber. "Turin, drive."

He started the car, and both men looked up and down the street. If they turn out to be innocent, I'd ask for forgiveness on my deathbed, but my gut told me they were with Mendoza and Dario.

"We should take them and get some information."

"I'm done talking." I rolled the window down as he

slowed and aimed the gun just as the back window of the car shattered. I fired a few shots before Turin floored the gas and took off.

"Damn it! They made us," I barked.

"I knew something was off." He shifted his gaze from the side to the rearview mirror.

Adding more bullets to my gun, I fired more shots. "Turn around."

"Axel, you have a death wish."

"Fuck!" I slammed my hand against the dashboard.

Turin made a sharp turn at the stop sign and got on the freeway.

I grumbled. "Hugo is pissing me off."

I reached in my pocket as my phone rang, seeing an unknown number.

"You were foolish tonight, boy," Hugo said.

"I won't make a mistake again."

"If you think you can get me, by all means, turn around."

I looked through the rearview mirror. "Get off the next exit," I ordered Turin.

Hugo chuckled. "I love playing games."

"All we want is Dario."

"All I want is Chicago and New York," Hugo replied.

"Greed only gets you death."

"We can have peace between our families," he suggested.

"Fuck you, Mendoza," I growled.

"The infamous Enforcer seems upset," he sneered.

"You took a shot. Now I'll take mine."

"Oh, I forgot to tell you. Dario says congrats on the new baby. He wondered if he should have gotten a DNA test, since some of his family's features could be present in Gaspare."

I gritted my teeth at the accusation. Gigi was a virgin when we got together. "Clearly, Dario wants to die slowly and painfully."

"I'm just the messenger," Hugo teased.

Thoughts of burning Dario alive assaulted me. "My wrath is not something you want to experience, Hugo."

"Then give me what I want," he demanded before hanging up.

Turin sped through the back streets to our home. He passed through the gates and stopped in front of the garage. I jumped out and rushed to the house. Running upstairs, I checked on Gaspare in his crib. The tension eased from my shoulders, and I sat in the rocking chair.

"Axel." Gigi's sweet voice came from the door, where she stood in her gown and robe.

The thought of my family being hurt was a weight on my heart. "Go back to bed."

Gigi crossed the threshold. "It's late."

Watching my son sleeping in his crib eased my anxiety. "I know. I had to take care of something."

"Something or someone? You look sweaty." Gigi strode to the crib and then turned to me.

"I made a move on Hugo."

She frowned. "Tonight?"

"Yeah."

Gigi rubbed Gaspare's stomach as he stirred. "Did they retaliate?"

My eyes dragged from her toes up to her face. She'd barely done anything, but she took my breath away like usual. "He will."

She sighed and moved to sit in my lap. I ran my hand up and down her back. "Tell me what happened?"

"I went to shoot at his people, and they made us first and shot out the window of Turin's car."

I held Gigi tightly as she went to jump out of my lap. "Is he all right?"

I nodded.

"Hugo and I should meet," Gigi stated plainly.

"Never."

"That's what he wants. To intimidate me and get you to falter."

I twirled the lace on her gown. "You will not be used as bait."

"Dario will come out of hiding if he sees I've made an agreement with Hugo," Gigi persisted.

"You're not giving Hugo anything." I cupped the back of her head.

"I've been thinking long and hard. Maybe we should let him have Chicago."

"Laurent would turn over in his grave."

Gigi stood. "It's my family's business."

I protested. "And your safety could be in jeopardy."

Gigi cupped my face. "Dario will make a stupid mistake if he sees Hugo fall in line with me."

"I hate the thought of Dario touching you."

"Baby, you're the man I want. Dario was only interested in me for selfish reasons. He backed down from his threat to harm me because of your intervention."

I grunted. "Let me think it over."

"I've decided, and it's final."

"So my opinion never mattered."

Gigi walked to the door. "I always take your opinions

into consideration, but you're clearly not thinking as the Enforcer, only as my husband."

She left. I contemplated her words and realized I agreed. All my choices had been from the perspective of a husband trying to keep his wife safe. Moves needed to be made on a bigger scale and Gigi was the link to everything.

Turin came into the house, so I went downstairs and met him in the kitchen while he was on the phone.

"Tomorrow, okay." Turin opened the fridge and passed a bottle of water to me. He ended the call and turned to me. "The two guys you shot at are still alive."

I leaned back on the island. "Fuck. That's all I need."

Turin tossed the lid of his water bottle in the garbage. "We'll worry about it later."

I repeated my conversation with Gigi. "She wants to meet with Hugo."

"Good." Turin said.

"I thought you agreed she was doing too much when she was pregnant."

Turin finished his water. "She was, and Hugo is dangling evidence that can hurt her and you."

"Do you think I'm doing right by her?"

Turin went to grab another water. "Gigi knows you'll take a bullet for her."

"When I asked her to step down, I think I feared she would be killed, like my parents."

"Being a husband and Enforcer will have your emotions conflicted."

"Sometimes I wish I'd stayed the Enforcer."

"Then you wouldn't have a family to come home to protect," Turin reminded me.

"The second we get Dario, I want him brought to me."

"There's a good chance we'll find him soon."

"Not soon enough, Turin. We've never been fucked over like this."

"My hands are tied, Axel. We're not in Italy and able to control movements."

"I know."

"Carlo and Antonio could help," Turin suggested.

"Can't ask them to get involved."

"It's a thought."

"Are you sleeping here?"

"I have Ralfie taking me home. We can chat later."

"Keep me posted, no matter the time of day." I walked him out and watched as he left with the second car of guards on standby.

I made sure the alarms were set and checked with the guard at the gate before turning out the lights. I headed upstairs and hopped in the shower to wash the night from my body. After drying off, I pulled on clean boxers and slid into bed next to a sleeping Gigi. I tugged her close and kissed the top of her forehead before giving in to sleep.

Chapter 8

Dario

Days turned into weeks and months of me staying under the radar until the right moment arrived. Today I knocked on the door of the hotel and waited as my nerves flipped my stomach around. Each calculation of my movements had made me public enemy number one to a lot of people, and the only hope I had left was on the other side of this door. The door opened wide, and his guard checked my pockets. I lifted my arms to show I didn't have anything on me.

"Come in, Mr. Ramini," Hugo called from the couch in the living room of his suite.

The man had bodyguards in his room and outside the building. I didn't know how much he paid them to not cause a fuss, but he was well protected.

I shook his hand and took a seat across from him. "Thank you for assisting me, Uncle."

"Well, as my godson, I did everything for you as a little boy in Italy. Your father was like a brother to me."

"My sincere appreciation goes out to you."

"Again, I give you my condolences over your family's

current fortunes." His words brought me back to Italy and how Axel and Gigi had destroyed my life.

"I plan on making the people pay."

"I trust you will because I'm here to help."

"The moment I found out the Carringtons killed Igor, I knew you'd want to get revenge."

Hugo nodded. "My nephew was a fuck up, but he was my only sister's boy and she misses him daily."

"Loss of family is hard."

"Tragic, but you're here with good news."

"I can get a meeting with the Irish cartel, the Murphys. All I want is protection and percentage."

After cutting the cigar, Hugo flicked the light at the end. "You plan on moving back to Italy?"

"I want what's rightfully mine. Ramini and Carrington joined as one."

"That will be difficult since Gigi is married to Axel."

"The minute I kill Axel and Gigi, I'm taking it back."

"Her men are loyal, aren't they?"

He offered me a cigar, but I declined. "Money and loyalty aren't the same thing to these men."

"She's a mother now. You tell me you don't care for her still?"

I shifted in my seat. "She's tainted by Axel now. I have no use for her."

"Your cousin and Raymond have been helpful."

A smirk spread across my face. "Amazing Gigi didn't look into them further or she would've discovered that he's Detective Alfeo Ramini Soren, my cousin. She fails at every step, yet still thinks she knows how to run a cartel."

"Soren dropping the Ramini name and taking his mother's last name worked for him," Hugo agreed.

"Is there anything else you need from me?" I asked.

"After Axel tried to kill my men the other night, and you got word of him following us, I was grateful."

"I only wish we'd killed him and Turin."

He put his cigar in the ashtray. "Give it time."

Hugo handed me a briefcase. "Here, take this for now, and I'll be in touch about the next meeting."

I opened it and saw hundreds of dollars wrapped for thousands. I took it from his grip and rose out of my chair. "You know where to find me."

Hugo grinned. "Tell your little friend we hope to see her one day for dinner."

I replied. "Ginerva would love that."

We shook hands, and I grinned as I left the hotel suite and took the elevator. All of my plans were slowly drawing close to the end of Gigi and Axel. The little bitch expected me to roll over and be okay with her making me look like a fool. It's why I took off the moment I got word about my father and called Igor and Hugo to get me to America to hide until I could come back full force.

The elevator stopped on the main floor, and I winked at the front clerk as I passed through the rolling doors.

I hurriedly hopped in the taxi waiting for me. "Back to the hotel you picked me up from."

"Sure thing." The driver left the meter running and moved into traffic to get back across town.

New York was a veritable melting pot to make a name for myself. I checked the time on my watch and looked out at the people who didn't have a clue about the corruption and evil that existed and controlled their lives. I popped the case open to run my hands over the money and closed it quickly as the driver stopped the car. I pulled some money from my pocket and pushed it in his hand.

* * *

I was bombarded as soon as I got through the door.

"Do you think he believed you?" Ginerva asked.

I ignored her question and went into the bedroom to transfer the money to my bag. Ginerva followed, watching as I zipped the bags and put them in the closet. She was annoyed because she'd had to stay here.

"Cheer up." I smacked her on the ass and stared while she fixed her blouse.

When Gigi heard her friend in distress months ago, I knew it would work in my favor. We'd already dealt with her family, and Gigi was worried about her best friend.

Ginerva and I had pretended to hate each other for years, all the while sleeping together. Gigi had no clue. Most times after I'd hung out with Gigi, I returned to Ginerva and we fucked the way I liked. Gigi wouldn't fuck before marriage and I had needs. None of the parents knew because took Ginerva outside the city to avoid any eyes on us.

Ginerva was ready to start a family, but I'd been putting it off until I had Gigi and Axel vanished from my life forever. After Laurent's death, my life changed dramatically. I knew I'd made mistakes that gave Gigi the opportunity to call off our engagement.

The Raminis had close ties with the Carringtons, and a family was at the least of my priorities. My father taught me that you needed money and power in the cartel world to get what you wanted. I would ensure Gigi suffered, knowing I took everything from her before I killed her.

"Can we go have lunch?" Ginerva asked.

"We can't be seen together."

She played with my tie. "We just went to the club."

"And I told you that was a one-time thing."

"Dario, why do we need to keep hiding? Gigi can't hurt us anymore," Ginerva challenged with a hiked brow.

Ginerva was clueless about me not having my full team or money besides what Hugo had given me for setting Axel up.

I clasped my hand around her throat and squeezed gently. "Gigi is slowly losing her power. Let me lead. Gigi made the same mistake, trying to dictate my moves."

Ginerva perched in my lap as I sat on the bed and wrapped her arms around my neck. "Fuck Gigi." She pushed her hand through my curly hair. I'd grown it out and had brown contacts when I first arrived in town.

"Give me a little more time."

"I miss my parents." She exhaled.

I pushed a strand of her hair away from her face. "You understand we had to leave."

Ginerva laid her head on my shoulder and grabbed my hand. She took a deep breath. "I need to tell you something, but I don't want you to get mad."

"What is it?"

"I saw Gigi at the mall." She chewed on a fingernail.

I pushed her off me and jumped up. "Repeat that again." I jammed my hands in my pockets.

"I forgot to tell you. When I went to the mall, she saw me and called my name, but I ran off."

I bent and gripped her jaw.

A sharp breath left her mouth. "Dario, you're hurting me."

"Shut the fuck up! I told you it was a bad idea to go out too early!" I shouted, releasing my hold.

"It'll be fine." Ginerva tried to grab the hem of my pants, and I shoved her away. "How do you know she didn't have anyone follow you back to the hotel?"

I stepped over her and looked out the window. We'd stayed in various hotels under different names as I wasn't ready to get an official home until I could put Axel in the ground. Gigi wouldn't be an easy kill compared to her husband. Now that she was a mother, it would be even more difficult to get her alone.

"I think she may have seen us at the bar the other night," Ginerva mumbled under her breath.

"I knew it was a mistake to go out that night."

She hung her head. "But you said all we needed to do was get Hugo on our side."

I cocked my head as I looked at her. "Hugo is only interested in what he can get out of the deal."

"He's your godfather," Ginerva argued, moving toward me.

"You're so naïve. That doesn't matter to a man like Hugo."

"I'm sorry, baby," she murmured, her eyes downcast as she leaned into me.

"I'll need to be extra cautious in the future."

"With the money Hugo gave you, we could find a place away from the city."

I took a deep breath and tried not to reveal my frustration. "That's the only good idea you've contributed so far."

Her chin rested on my chest as she purred, "Dario, I love you."

"Then start using your brain, Ginerva! One thing you have in common with Gigi is the fuck-ups."

Ginerva stamped her foot in a fit of temper. "I'm nothing like her!"

"Go order room service. I need to make a call." Moving away, I took my phone off the charger and dialed Alfeo's number.

"Fine." Ginerva pouted and stomped out of the bedroom.

"Cousin, any news?" I closed the bedroom door to talk in private.

Alfeo answered, "We installed trackers on two of her vehicles so we know where she is at all times."

"Good. I met with Hugo and he's laid out his plan."

Alfeo hissed, "You know we can't have any dealings with him and shouldn't be talking over the phone."

"I agree. Let's meet." I looked at the time on my watch. "Same hotel?"

I gazed around the room. "Yeah, but I might be moving out of here today."

"What happened?"

"Ginerva confessed that Gigi saw her at the mall."

"How the fuck did that happen?"

From the window, I looked around the parking lot's surroundings. "A long story. We should meet now." I pulled out the bag from the closet and took a few dollars.

"Raymond's caught up with a case right now. It'll just be me."

"Fine."

"Go to the park on Flushing Meadows in Queens."

"See you soon." The call ended, and I left the room.

Ginerva appeared with the hotel phone and the room

service menu. I kissed her and explained I'd be back in a little while. I placed the bag in the safe and gave her some to pay for the room. Everything was cash to be safe.

$$* * *$$

"Alfeo." I tossed my head back to signal it was me alone, with my guards near the car.

Alfeo shook my hand, and we talked while we walked while a few parents and their kids played.

"So far, I've got a few photos of Gigi going out with the wife of the De Luca Cartel and attending a few doctor appointments."

"How did she take it when you showed up at her home?" I flipped through the pictures of Gigi laughing and a few of her holding her son.

Alfeo responded, "She was pissed, as you'd expect."

"Ginerva told me she saw us at the nightclub?" Despite his shorter stature and different complexion, we had the same shaped noses and round eyes that showed the family resemblance.

"I tried to get close to her, but her friends jumped in and pulled her away.

"We made a mistake going there."

His expression grew serious. "Told you to move to another country until things cool off."

"They killed most of my family. I'm not giving them the satisfaction of running away."

He eyed me critically. "Dragging that bitch Ginerva with you will get you caught."

I glared at him. "I have love for her, and she's loyal."

"Loyal and dumb, cousin."

I waved him off.

"Listen to me, the only reason you're not dead is because of Hugo and me," he challenged.

"You're getting something out of the deal." I scanned the area to ensure nobody was watching. Reaching into my pocket, I pulled out a stack of money and passed it to him.

His brown eyes burned into mine. "I put my career on the line, so money is the least you could do. You're family, but I don't give blind loyalty."

I ignored his statement. "Anything else you've found?"

He lowered his voice. "Axel may go after Hugo following the ambush at the warehouse."

"Shit." I cursed as the walls closed in on me.

Alfeo soke harshly. "If he does, it will link to me, and I'm not going down alone."

"Will Raymond fold?" His people's loyalty was crucial to me.

"Doubt it, but you never know when life in prison or death are the only options," Alfeo replied.

"Okay, keep me updated, and I'll keep the money flowing. I want Gigi and Axel dead."

"All I can do is provide the setup. My hands are tied when it comes to pulling the trigger." Alfeo strolled away.

One day, I'd claim my rightful position as Boss of a cartel.

Chapter 9

Ginerva

inerva! Ginerva!"

"G I'd been stuck in hotel after hotel for months, and the day I finally convince Dario to let me spend a little time at the mall, I almost get caught by Gigi. The moment I heard her voice that day, I knew it was her. But I felt if she'd caught me, it would've been the end of Dario and me. He's the only man I've ever loved, and Gigi didn't deserve him.

The engagement my parents arranged for me was the last straw, and I decided to go all in on Dario's plan to escape and start a new life together in public. But he'd forced me to stay behind these closed doors. I felt caged in and wondered what could have been if I had gone with my first choice to tell Gigi the truth about our relationship. Dario forbade me from telling Gigi the first time we had sex after one of their fights. Dario came across as tough, but he was a sweetheart to me and spoiled me with gifts and dinners, plus trips. I wanted the wedding and children, and he'd promised we would be married with our own house the minute all of this was over.

"I can have Raymond and Soren send over the photos." He was still on the phone when he walked back into the hotel again hours later. Hours that had left me bored by myself watching tv. I came in from the balcony and shut the door. Sitting on the couch, I watched him pour his second drink of the day from the bar. His constant drinking was a new thing. I'd brought it up a few times, but he only got angry and snatched it out of my hands when I tried to toss it in the sink.

He stared at me while continuing his phone conversation. "We can have dinner. I'll bring her."

I crossed my leg and waited. When Dario finished his call, he put the phone into his pocket and took a sip of his drink as he approached me.

I almost gagged when I smelled the liquor on his breath. "I missed you today."

His hand felt clammy as he touched me. "Ginerva don't start."

He removed his hand and sat beside me on the couch, picking up the remote.

The thought of him being with another woman made me jealous. "Don't you start."

"Baby, it was a long day of tying up loose ends." He stretched his arm along the back of the couch, leaning in to place a kiss behind my ear.

Persuasion was my goal. "I want to get out of this hotel." I turned my head and caught his kiss.

"The last time you almost got caught," Dario murmured through the kiss.

"It won't happen again," I promised.

"Let me think about it."

I jerked back. "No. I want my nails done. Maybe a spa day."

"They have a spa here in the hotel."

"Everything is about the damn hotel. I'm over being stuck in here, Dario!"

"Sit down," Dario demanded.

I refused, and he gripped the remote, throwing it at the wall and getting up in my face. "Bitch, sit your spoiled ass down."

I slapped his face. "Fuck you, Dario!" I was over his demands.

His hand flashed out, and he backhanded me, knocking me to the ground.

"You hit me!" I gasped in shock.

He grabbed my hair and yanked my head back. "I love you, Ginerva, but you're acting more and more like Gigi."

"That doesn't give you the right to put your hands on me."

"Baby, calm down."

"No. Let me go." I tried to remove his hand from my hair.

He kissed me on the lips, and I pushed him back. "I hate you!" I'd never had to deal with being abused by a man.

Regret crossed his face as he helped me up. "I'm sorry, Ginerva. I promise I'll never do it again. I need you to get dressed. We have dinner plans."

"Not going." My cheeks tingled with tears as I argued.

"It's important." He led me back to the couch and sat beside me.

I threw my hands in the air. "Again, all about you."

He groaned and stood. "If you come with me tonight, I'll let you pick out the house with the realtor."

I looked at him in amazement. "You found a house?"

He nodded. "That's one of the things I did today."

A part of me trusted him and I'd gone along with his excuses for the past few months. "Who's dinner with tonight?"

"Hugo Mendoza."

"Your God uncle?"

He nodded and nudged me toward the bedroom. I stood in front of my luggage and contemplated if I should continue or leave. He cupped my face, and I winced from where he'd slapped me.

"I'm sorry, baby. Please forgive me." He kissed my forehead.

I poked his chest. "If you touch me in the wrong way again, I'm leaving you, Dario."

He lifted my hand to his mouth and kissed my palm. "I hear you, baby."

* * *

"Ginerva, I hear you and my godson have been in love for years and plan to get married soon." Hugo cut into his steak.

With a gulp, I poured more wine into my empty glass. "Dario knows I want babies and marriage."

Dario stretched his arm around my shoulder at the table. The restaurant wasn't too far from the hotel. I fiddled with my plate of squash and liver.

"Hugo, thank you again for handling our little problem. I met with my cousin, and he's on board."

"Does he know what I want?" Hugo asked.

Dario rubbed his hands together. "He does, and we'll have a clear chance soon to lock you in for New York."

"Which cousin?" I asked.

Hugo raised an eyebrow. "She doesn't know everything, does she?"

"I thought it best to leave out certain details."

I frowned. "Dario, what are you hiding?"

He leaned over and kissed my cheek. "We can talk later."

I felt like a child being patted on the head. "Excuse me." I rose from the chair, dropped my napkin on the table, and picked up my purse.

"Where are you going?" Dario snarled.

"To the bathroom, if that's all right with you?" I snapped.

Dario pointed at his hired goon. "Take the guard with you."

"I'll be fine going to the bathroom." I started to walk off, but he gripped my hand.

"Take the bodyguard, honey."

I sighed. "Fine. Let's go."

He was pissing me off. I wanted to be included in all the decisions, and he was keeping me out of the loop. He didn't trust me, and that made me feel like Gigi.

I stood at the mirror in the bathroom and checked my hair and makeup. I'd applied my makeup thickly to cover the bruising on my face.

A toilet flushed and a beautiful woman stepped out of the cubicle. She smiled as she approached me. "Long night with the boyfriend?"

I chuckled. "Is it obvious?"

"I've been there before, and now he's my husband." She laughed.

"The goal is to get him to propose." I fixed my hair.

She washed her hands and grabbed paper towels to dry them.

"Give him time. Pushing will make him run off. I know from experience." She smiled and left the bathroom.

A few minutes later, I emerged to find Dario waiting outside the door.

He snatched my arm. "What the fuck did you do?"

"Dario, have you been drinking?" I threw off his hand.

"Shut up and let's go." He grabbed my arm again and pushed me to the back exit.

"What's wrong? I didn't finish my food."

Dario shoved me against the car door. "Did you tell her anything?"

"Who?"

"Dammit, this could be bad." He yanked the door open.

I snatched my arm away again. "I'm not leaving until you tell me."

"Janice Russo, the wife of Carlo Russo and best friend of Antonio De Luca."

My body tensed at the statement. "You're certain it was her?"

"In my line of work, you need to know all the players, and for the third time, you've fucked us over."

"She doesn't know me." His paranoia has returned.

"Carlo knows Hugo and me. I know them from my family's business. Get in the fucking car so we can go." His face flushed as he sneered.

He shoved me to the back door, and I climbed in with

tears falling down my cheeks. I knew love took sacrifices, but we barely held a conversation.

"Do you really think she recognized me?"

His guard shut the door. "Stop talking, Ginerva."

"Dario, you can't blame me for everything that has gone wrong."

He rubbed his forehead. "Give me a minute to think."

"Where did Hugo go?"

"He took off as soon as I pointed out Carlo leaving with Janice." Dario slammed his elbow against the window.

"Maybe it was too dark, and they didn't see us."

Dario ignored me and picked up his vibrating phone, sending messages back and forth.

"We can't hide anymore," I said.

"All the pieces aren't in place for me to reveal myself," Dario argued.

"Maybe I can help," I suggested.

"How?" Dario mocked.

Maybe she would call a truce. "Let me contact Gigi."

"No." He stuffed the cell into his pocket.

"Listen, it would work because she's not expecting me to be here in America."

He paused and stared at me. Finally, he was paying attention to me without being distracted by an argument or sex.

"Gigi would be vulnerable. She'd let me come to her place. I could tell her how I escaped and used my savings to fly here to start fresh."

"No. Too dangerous," he stated as we headed down Atlantic Ave.

I extended my hand and touched his arm. "Baby, I need to help. It'll work. Let me do something."

"Let me think about it first." Dario rubbed his chin.

I kissed him on the lips and grinned.

Dario was pulling all the strings, but I had a few ideas that could work and take care of our Gigi and Axel problem much sooner. There were others who could lead cartels and be wives besides Gigi. Obviously, it would take time, but with me beside him, we'd be richer and safer.

Chapter 10

Gigi

I was hesitant to go to the main office. It sprinkled with rain this morning when Gaspare woke up around six. I fed him and spent some time with him before deciding to go into the office to check on the status of the business.

The conference room was silent, and all eyes were on me. Our top soldiers were present, along with our accountant and bodyguards. I hadn't been gone that long. Our drops were being made, and the money was rolling in.

Axel had an appointment with the doctor to check on his progress, although he'd tried to get out of it to be here. I demanded he went and told him I'd fill him in afterward.

"Thank you for coming, gentleman. I know we have a lot of work you need to oversee, so I won't keep you long."

We used Oliver's club to distribute our products since he was one of our top suppliers and the low-level Boss of the cartel. "How are we protecting our spots?"

"Hoboken is a hot spot, and our most profitable location," Oliver said.

"We will rebuild, but until then, a bigger problem has come about," I reported.

"Oliver's right, we need answers if we're going to talk to our men." Another soldier spoke, interrupting my thoughts.

"I'll fire the next person who tells me what I should be doing," I snapped. "Dario Ramini is trying to come after my business."

"Mrs. Bresciani, nice to see your entire crew here," a recognizable voice observed.

My head swiveled to see Detectives Soren and Raymond standing in the doorway. "How did you get in here?"

"Our badges mean something to security," Raymond replied.

We handled legit real estate, shipping, and importing, but a large portion of our time was spent on cartel business. "This is my office. We're a legitimate company."

Detective Soren stepped into the room, looking at the certificates of major deals hanging on the walls. "Doing what?" Soren inquired.

"Real estate, shipping, and investments."

"I highly doubt you're into investments," Detective Soren said as pulled out a chair and sat in front of me.

I raised an eyebrow at his boldness. "This is a private meeting."

"Please don't let us interrupt." Soren sat back with his hands clasped together.

"Do you have a warrant?" I reached for the phone on the desk.

"Is a warrant needed?" A smirk crossed Detective Soren's face.

I bent to look him in the eye, placing my hands on the

table. "I doubt you'd be here wasting your time on a wild goose chase."

My men glared at the detectives. If I snapped my fingers, they'd make them disappear, but that would be falling into their trap.

"It's quite simple. You run a major drug and weapons cartel." Detective Raymond jumped into the conversation.

"I run an investment and real estate business," I repeated.

"Are you telling me all these men sell homes?" Soren pointed around the room at my guys.

Our cartel had a dress code that my father implemented years ago to be professional at all times, even with the legit business we handled. "Get out of my office and building." I waved for my guards to escort the cops out.

"I need you to come down to the station," Detective Soren stated.

I rose from my seat and folded my arms. "Why?"

"We'd like to ask you a few questions about the death of Igor Mendoza."

"I've answered all of your questions about Mendoza."

"Humor me." Soren stood and gestured for me to leave with him.

I stared around the room and knew it would only make me look worse if I denied his request. I nodded, grabbed my purse and jacket from my chair, and sauntered out of the conference room.

Raymond pushed the elevator button as I removed my phone to text my lawyer. It was a relief to know that Gaspare was home with the nanny and Ebony.

I shoved the phone back in my purse. "My lawyer will meet us there."

"A lawyer?" a disappointed Detective Soren asked, his mouth a tight line of disapproval.

"Yes, my lawyer. I'm not some stupid little woman you can manipulate."

He grinned as the elevator pinged.

"Unless you're feeling guilty," Detective Raymond said, holding the elevator door open for me to step out.

I raised my hand to stop the security as they approached.

"Guys, I'll be fine. Just a routine visit. Nothing to worry about."

"Mrs. Bresciani, are you sure?" one of them asked.

"Yes. Please lock the doors early today."

"Our car is right out front," Detective Raymond said.

"That won't be necessary. My driver will follow you." I pointed at Ralfie standing at my town car.

I smirked as Soren's jaw ticked with disapproval. "After you, Detective Soren." They probably thought I'd get in the car blindly and end up in some ditch, dead and beaten. Soren thought the cartel world was a new toy for me, but he'd forgotten I was Laurent Carrington's daughter.

* * *

Soren pulled the chair out. "Have a seat, Mrs. Bresciani."

"Why is my client here, detectives?" my lawyer, John Flair, demanded.

It was Detective Soren's turn to ask the question. "Mrs. Bresciani was seen at a hotel in Chicago with Igor Mendoza, a well-known mob Boss."

John flicked through pictures he'd been given from

the hotel. "My client visits hotels all the time. Nothing wrong with that."

"He was seen going into her room," Detective Soren said.

"Then we should contact the hotel about him entering her room without her permission."

Soren glared at John. "Nice try, but we know Igor Mendoza and the Carrington Cartel are enemies."

"Any evidence of this?" John challenged.

Raymond and Soren exchanged a glance.

"No? Then we have no reason to be here." John closed the folder.

Soren frowned. "Igor Mendoza's death is international news. If Mrs. Bresciani wants to live a long life, she should confess to the killing and we might be able to help her."

"Are you threatening me?" I sat forward in my seat.

Soren fixed his tie. "I'm trying to help you, Gigi."

I chastised. "Mrs. Bresciani to you, Detective Soren."

His brows pulled together.

"Our only goal is to find the killer. Now would be a good time for her to tell us anything she knows." Detective Raymond pointed at me.

"Is there any evidence that shows her at the scene?" John asked.

Soren clenched his fists and watched me intently. He had to know it was me.

"She's free to go for now," Soren told us.

I stood and collected my things.

"Next time, make sure you have a warrant and concrete evidence."

"You're right about one thing," Soren said.

"What?" John asked.

"There will be a next time," Soren replied.

He made me uneasy, and I wanted to punch him in his smug face.

"Do I need to know anything, Gigi?" John asked as he pulled me away from the station.

. I shook my head. "Nothing to tell."

John faced me. "As your lawyer—-"

"Let me stop you right there, John. I didn't do anything."

"Keep your hands clean."

"If Detective Soren makes another move, I can't promise that my husband will keep *his* hands clean."

"Keep your voice down. We're still inside a police station, so making threats isn't appropriate."

"John, that wasn't a veiled threat. It was a suggestion to ensure the police stay out of my place of business."

We shook hands, and I got back in the car and headed home.

My phone rang, and I quickly grabbed it from my purse to see an unknown number.

"Hello?" I heard heavy breathing.

"Gigi?" a soft voice asked.

"Who is this?"

"Gigi, it's me."

"I think you have the wrong number." I started to hang up.

"It's Geneva."

My chest tightened. "Ginerva?"

"It's really me," she replied. "Gigi, can we meet?"

My hand flew to my mouth in shock as my phone beeped with another incoming call. "I...I... can't believe it."

"I know. I'd like to meet and talk."

"Hold on, I have another call." I pulled the phone away from my ear and clicked over in time to hear Janice shouting in the background.

"Janice, what's up?"

Janice released a breath. "Oh, thank god you answered."

"I'm leaving the police station now."

Confusion and concern from Janice. "The police station? How come?"

"A long story."

"Where's Axel?"

"He had a doctor's appointment today."

"Well, Carlo wanted me to wait for him to tell you both at the same time," Janice continued.

"Tell me what?"

"Are you almost home?" she asked, avoiding my question.

"Yeah, in about five minutes."

"I'll stop by and talk to you in person."

"Janice, you're scaring me. Ginerva is on the other line."

"The best friend who went missing?"

"Yes, and I need to call you back."

"Don't get off this phone with me," Janice pleaded urgently.

"Janice, you're not making sense."

"I know, but Carlo wants me to tell you and Axel at the same time."

"Can you give me a hint?"

"It has something to do with Dario."

"How do you know?"

She hushed her kids in the background. "Just act

normal when you get back on the phone with her. I promise to explain as soon as you get home."

"I feel like you're keeping secrets from me."

"Gigi, as your friend, believe me, I will explain when you get home."

"Okay, the car is driving through the gate now."

"Give me a few minutes to get the kids settled."

"Sure. Talk later."

The car pulled into the driveway, and Ralfie opened the passenger door.

I clicked back over to Ginerva. "Hey, Minerva."

Ginerva chuckled. "Thank goodness you didn't hang up."

I removed my key from my purse and unlocked the door. "Um, how did you get to America? I mean, you are in New York, right?"

"I'll explain everything when I see you.

I smiled. "I'm a mother and wife now."

"We have a lot to catch up on."

"Where are you staying?" I removed my jacket and strode into the living room to see Axel holding Gaspare. I threw my jacket on the couch, along with my purse, and slipped my feet out of my heels.

"In the city. I'll text you the details. And Gigi?"

"Yes?"

"You're still my best friend."

My heart was filled with a familiar joy. "Me too."

Axel gave me a perplexed look. "Who was that?"

"Geneva."

"She's alive? You're positive?"

"I know! Can you believe it?" I asked in shock, tossing my phone aside.

"You okay?" Axel pulled me into his arms.

I placed a hand on Gaspare's back as he squirmed in his father's arms. "Janice called me on the way home."

"I heard about your visit to the police station from John."

The fireplace was lit and Gaspare's toys were strewn on the floor. "He knows I killed Igor."

"Soren can't prove anything," Axel reassured me.

"If one of the staff sold a copy of the video, he has me on tape."

"He won't be able to show it to anyone." Axel held me close.

The front doorbell chimed. "That's Janice."

"Turin is here. We had a meeting with Carlo and Antonio."

I smoothed my hand along his arm. "How did it go with the doctors?"

"I'm fine."

"Axel." He was as stubborn as my father when it came to his health. It was always a struggle to convince him to go to the doctor.

"Seriously, he told me to continue with what I've been doing and not overwhelm myself."

"So that means no overexertion."

Janice walked in with Turin right at the same time. "Hey, you two."

I took Gaspare from Axel and kissed his chubby cheek. "You sounded worried on the phone."

Janice put her purse down on the table and sat on the chair. "Did Carlo tell you?" She directed her question to Axel.

"Tell him what?" I asked as Janice and Axel exchanged a look.

"Gigi, I need you to listen to me and not interrupt," Janice said.

"What is this about?"

Axel placed a hand on my thigh. "Ginerva."

"Okay."

"The other night I saw Geneva with Dario," Janice said.

I blinked, not comprehending her words. "What did you say?"

"Ginerva was on a date with Dario and another guy called Hugo Mendoza."

My eyes went wide. "Ginerva would never be around Dario."

"She was," Axel answered.

"How...?"

"Carlo told me before you arrived. I waited to tell you tonight, but Janice contacted you first. You were already on the phone with Ginerva, which confirmed what we already knew."

I shook my head in disbelief. "Are you saying Ginerva is sleeping with Dario?"

The way they looked at the table, I would say they're lovers, and have been for a while," Janice replied.

None of this made sense. "Ginerva hates Dario. I think your eyes were playing tricks on you."

"Carlo told me Hugo Mendoza and Dario were talking, and the girl got up and left for the bathroom. I met her in the bathroom when I came out."

"But-"

Janice continued to explain. "I didn't know her at first, but Carlo reminded me about your best friend."

"He must have forced her."

"Didn't look like force to me. She talked about getting

a proposal from him. Even with a bruise on her right eye she tried to cover up with bad makeup," Janice said.

"He hit her!"

"Probably more, but I didn't have time to probe because Carlo noticed them and wanted to leave. I didn't want to get too involved, because she looked like a puppy in love."

"She asked to meet with me," I whispered.

"Probably to set you up," Turin announced, reminding me he was in the room.

I whispered to myself, "She would never betray me like Rosa."

"You can't meet her alone," Janice stated.

"Hugo is working with Dario and the detectives," Axel said grimly.

"We got the footage from the office today of them entering the building," Turin confirmed.

"Keep Oliver and the other guys on high alert," Axel told Turin.

"What are you going to do?" Janice asked.

As the love in my heart for my former friend faded, I let the memories fade with it. "I have to meet with Ginerva."

"I'm coming," Axel replied.

I figured. "It'll tip Dario off if you come."

"She's right," Turin agreed.

"Turin can come with me," I said.

"That's more reason Dario will stay away," Axel insisted.

"He'd probably feel secure knowing I had a guard or two with me."

"We'll talk about it later," Axel said. He stood and left the living room.

"Can you watch him? I need to talk to Axel." I handed Gaspare to Janice.

Axel was overly protective, and if anything went wrong, he'd burn the world down to find Dario. But I didn't need him doing anything that would cause Gaspare and me to lose him for good. The explosion was enough and still gave me nightmares. Going into labor without him next to me was a subject I never brought up, but I knew he had guilt. Honestly, being selfish, I wanted him to feel that guilt. Marriage wasn't rainbows and flowers. I'd had to grow up sooner than I wanted, but the person I married was the love of my life, and I had to get him to see me for who I was now. I pushed his office door open and saw him with his back to the door, staring at a picture of his parents on the wall.

"How can I make it better?" I asked, coming up behind him.

"I'm not the same person as before. They took months away from me."

"I know." I was resigned to the situation, but I wanted Axel to be at peace.

He turned around and glared. "Do you?"

I groaned. "Axel—"

He threw his hand up to stop me. "My instinct is to and kill anything that brings you pain. I'd never hesitate. Every minute, I find myself more worried about you and Gaspare's safety at."

"That's a part of being a parent."

"No, it's crippling, Gigi. Sometimes I wish I would have died."

"Axel, don't think like that."

"I lived and breathed being Enforcer for the family.

Now, I second guess myself. I'm not confident that you still love me like before."

I ran into his arms. "Where is this coming from? I've never stopped loving you."

He grasped my hips. "We haven't been together as husband and wife. I missed seven months of your life. It feels like we're starting all over again."

"I had a baby, and you're still dealing with what happened. Getting back to us as a couple will come in stages. We have to be patient."

He kissed my forehead. "I'm not used to waiting. On top of my enemies being this close to us."

"I won't go to see Ginerva if you don't want me to."

He buried his face in my neck and inhaled. "I want to touch you."

"Okay."

"I want to bury my dick so far inside you, you're all I can feel."

"Yes," I moaned as he squeezed my ass.

Axel mumbled, "Shit, I want you so bad."

"My six weeks are up. But I want to check with the doctor."

"I can tell you if you're healed."

I chuckled and shook my head. "Baby, no. Let me talk to the doctor. Getting pregnant right after Gaspare is not in my plans."

"If it happens, I'll be here."

"You promise?" I brushed my tongue across his lips.

He groaned. "Fuck, yes."

"One more day. I'll make an emergency appointment."

"Gigi—"

"One more day, handsome."

Axel and I made out for the next ten minutes until Turin knocked on the door. He announced he was leaving and would be back to figure out the plan about Ginerva.

Chapter 11

Axel

My back was a little sore from working out, but I pushed through to complete the work-out. I wiped my brow and sipped on the protein shake as I walked into my office for a meeting with Turin. I lifted the folder from my desk and took a seat.

Turin checked his gun. "Are you sure you're ready for today?"

I closed the folder. "I'm ready. I just need to shower."

Turin nodded. "As your brother, I have to check."

"Did you get Onyx for today?"

"He's here."

I placed the folder on the desk and headed for the shower.

Some of our soldiers were hand-picked to be on point when Gigi went to meet with Ginerva. They were the best trained assassins the cartel had.

The folder Turin obtained from surveillance showed Ginerva was in the club with Dario. On a couple of occasions, she'd also been there alone with a guard. She'd been here for months and had lied to Gigi. It would take more than killing her and Dario to make me feel whole again. I wanted to wipe out her entire bloodline in Italy.

Hugo had scheduled a meeting with the Irish today. I planned on crashing it to reinforce that the Carringtons owned the territory Hugo was trying to take. The Irish were only loyal to themselves, and Hugo would learn not to cross my wife or me again.

Once I was showered and dressed, I headed back to my office and grabbed two guns and some money from the safe. Gigi had an appointment with her doctor for an update and even if she wasn't at the six-week mark, it was time to be with my wife.

Turin was waiting outside with the car.

"Hugo is to be left alive," I stated.

"What if Dario is there?" Onyx asked.

"He won't step foot near the deal," Turin explained.

Onyx frowned. "How can you be sure?"

"Ginerva," I replied.

"He's banking on Gigi seeing Ginerva, so he'll lie low," Turin explained.

"You two take the rear. Turin and I will be up front," I instructed.

"I'll drive," Turin announced.

"What if the Irish get involved?" Onyx asked.

I shrugged. "Kill them."

I walked to the Jeep and climbed in. Arriving in a limo would draw too much attention, and the Jeep had better maneuverability to get us out of a situation unharmed. It was bulletproof, so no more ambushes unless we were the ones doing them.

Turin drove for fifteen minutes in silence. The guys checked and rechecked their guns, and I blocked out everyone except Hugo's face as my target. Finally, we approached the restaurant where Hugo was planning to meet with the Russians, and we climbed out and walked to the back door. It was opened by one of the servers Turin had paid off to get us inside.

"They just got here," he said.

Turin handed him a thousand dollars. "You never saw us."

"Saw who?" He grinned and ran out the door.

No one was back here, so we had a clear path of the hallway to the bathrooms. Onyx checked them, but they were empty. Turin followed behind him.

I waited before moving forward. "You on the right. I'll take the left," I whispered to Turin.

"Gotcha—"

Bullets came flying in our direction before we could move. We took cover and backed up out of the building in a rush.

"Fuck!"

I fired off two shots, but only saw a server down on the ground.

"Time to go. They made us!" Turin yelled.

I refused to leave. "No."

Gunfire exploded, and Turin pushed me out of the way, taking the bullet meant for me.

"Turin!"

"Shit! We need to get him to a doctor!" Onyx shouted.

We hauled Turin to his feet between us.

"I'm good. Shit... my shoulder," Turin groaned.

"Start the car, Onyx." I shoved the keys into his hand.

I helped Turin into the backseat while our other men watched our backs, providing cover from the gunfire.

"Let's get the fuck out of here!" Onyx ripped the door open, slid into the driver's seat, and started the engine as

Mendoza's men emerged from the building. I pulled my cell from my pocket and dialed Gigi's number.

No answer.

I redialed her number.

"Take the smaller streets..." Turin's head fell on my shoulder.

I dropped my phone and tapped him on the cheek to stay awake. "Turin, hold on. We're almost there."

"We can't go to the hospital. Too many questions!" Onyx swerved in and out of traffic.

"Get to my house. I'll take care of everything," I ordered.

Onyx sped up, ignoring the red light and cutting off a cab.

"Stay awake," I told Turin.

"Fuck, I'm good. Just a flesh wound," Turin replied.

Neither of us were doctors, but it looked worse than a flesh wound.

Onyx made it to the house. The guards opened the door and helped Turin out while I dialed Gigi again.

"Put him in the guest house," I barked as the nurse, Heather, stepped out of the house.

"Mr. Bresciani, we had a scheduled appointment today."

"I need your help."

"Missing appointments won't help your recovery."

"Come with me." I grabbed her hand and led her to the guesthouse.

"Wait a minute! What's going on?"

"No time to explain. I need you to help my friend."

"But—"

"We can't take him to the hospital. Too many questions."

"Sir, I'm not a doctor."

"Then do what you can to keep him alive."

"How bad is it?"

"He's lost a lot of blood." I opened the door to reveal Turin lying on the couch, holding his arm.

Heather ran over and lifted his shirt to reveal another bullet wound on his right side. "He needs a hospital."

"Do what you can to keep him alive. I have someone who might be able to help."

"I need my bag."

I motioned for one of my guards to go to the main house and grab her things. Stepping outside, I ran my hand through my hair and released a shaky breath.

"He's going to make it." Onyx came to stand next to me.

"Hugo's going to pay."

"He's gotten the jump on us twice."

"Won't be a third." I stalked to the garage, opened the door, and stood back in thought.

"What are you doing?" Onyx squinted at me.

"Checking the cars."

"For what?" Onyx wondered.

"A tracker."

I went to the Mercedes, limo, and Lamborghini and found the same small black box underneath the wheel well. I stomped on each one and threw them in the trash.

Onyx rushed toward the other two-door garage. "You won't believe what the fuck I found."

He removed a device from the front wheel of the BMW that Gigi drove and held up the same black tracker.

* * *

Once we'd swept the cars clean, I had Onyx take me to my doctor. We needed discretion, and the only person I could think of was Dr. Nathaniel.

"Mr. Bresciani, I'm a doctor. I can't be involved with this," he said anxiously as we sat in his office.

"Is this your family?" I indicated the picture frame on his desk.

"Yes, my wife and daughter."

"You love your family?"

"What kind of question is that?"

"Just answer the question."

"I do."

"Turin is my brother. One of only two people I trust in this world."

"I understand your friend is hurt."

I raised my gun and pointed it at his face. "Come with me willingly or forcefully."

"I could lose my license."

"No one will know. It's a house call."

He dropped his head in defeat.

"All right, Doc. We only have a few minutes to get Turin some help," Onyx added.

"You will be compensated," I added.

"I don't want your money."

"Even better." I stood and tucked my gun away.

"Fine. Let me tell my staff."

"No. Give me your phone."

"What? I need to be able to contact my staff and family."

"Soon as Turin is stable, you'll get your phone back." I wiggled my fingers for him to pass it to me.

The doctor lifted his medical bag and jacket, then reached into his pocket and took out his cell.

"The pager as well," I said.

"What makes you think I won't talk after I help your friend?"

"Because your family will be under surveillance for the rest of your lives. If I get one inkling of police at my door, you can kiss your wife goodbye."

We made it back to the house as Heather stepped out of the guesthouse, wiping her hands clean of blood. "Doctor Nathaniel?"

"You've been pulled into this mess, too?" Nathaniel asked.

I pushed him toward the guest house. "Another time, Doc."

"What is he doing here?" Heather demanded.

"Work. Go assist him and keep your mouth shut about what you've seen here."

"This isn't the way." Heather rolled her eyes.

"I learned a long time ago that life doesn't play fair."

They worked on Turin for hours. I stood watch as they removed the bullets and cleaned the wounds. I marched out of the guest house, leaving Onyx to guard them, and went into the main house to find Gigi asleep in bed. I kissed her on the forehead and went into the bathroom to shower and change.

Forty minutes into my sleep, I felt kisses on my neck and chest as Gigi pressed her body against mine.

"Gigi," I whispered. She was my calm, the cure I needed when my head was clouded. "I missed you all day."

I pulled her leg over my thigh as my dick probed at her opening and brushed my thumb over the soft pillow of her bottom lip.

"Axel, we shouldn't," Gigi moaned.

"Why not?" I wound a lock of her hair around my finger.

"What if I get pregnant again before I fully heal?"

"I'll pull out." I rocked her back and forth slowly.

Gigi leaned forward and kissed me on the lips. "I missed us together."

My fingers slowly pushed forward into her pussy, and she dug her nails into my shoulder. "I had a rough day and I need you," I groaned.

"Yes, right there." She lifted her hips in invitation.

I captured her lips and held her there as I devoured her tongue, then pushed into her warm, tight pussy.

"Axel," she breathed, tossing her head back.

"I'll go slow, baby."

She dipped her head, avoiding eye contact while I did all the work to make us both comfortable. She wasn't the only one who was nervous. This was our first time since the car bomb. My heart beat faster and sweat dripped down my forehead. I moved my hands over her back and smacked her ass before flipping her onto her back.

Gigi cried out. "Axel, I missed you."

"Tell me again."

Gigi laid her palm on my chest. "I missed you. You feel so good."

I cupped her stomach. "I missed your first appointment with the doctor when you were growing our baby."

"It's okay." Gigi covered my hand with hers.

I shook my head. "It will never be okay. You're mine to care for and protect."

Heat spread to her cheeks at my words. I smoothed my hands up her arms, bringing her closer and locking her into my embrace. My mouth covered hers hungrily. I fondled her plump breast and tasted her sweet nipple while I stroked slowly inside her. The pleasure was pure, out of this world.

"I'll always be yours," she panted.

I covered her mouth with mine to capture her screams as she flew over the edge. I stroked into her twice more before I released and fell on top of her. I knew she'd be pissed about me not pulling out, but I couldn't move.

Gigi's arms locked around me and she whimpered, "I love you."

Her words gave me hope we would be okay once our enemies were dead.

I started to thrust again. "Fuck those six weeks."

She bit my shoulder as I sucked on her nipple, and we lost ourselves in each other.

* * *

Days passed. I was running on adrenaline and focused on ending anyone who came after my family. In the mornings, I had breakfast with Gigi and Gaspare and after a few days of hanging around the house, I made plans to meet Antonio at his club, Ryde.

The liquor cabinet was the first place he went as we sat in his nightclub while Carlo stood at the door.

Antonio had his back to me. Carlo told the staff they'd be unavailable for a few hours while we met. I rubbed the back of my neck, still sore as I'd pushed myself hard in physical therapy.

Antonio said, "I don't like what I'm seeing in my city."

"What have you heard?" I asked.

Antonio sat at his desk and pushed a glass in front of me. "Hugo Mendoza is trying to take over."

My throat burned with panic. De Luca starting a war

with Mendoza when we already had the Irish trying to gain footing would cut into our profits. Gigi had done well to manage and expand the business because of the friendship we had with Antonio and Carlo.

"It's true." I informed him.

Antonio tapped his finger against his glass. "He's gotten too close."

"A plan is in the works to get him," I said.

"What about the Irish?" Carlo asked.

"Unless they can get Hugo, they'll probably want a lower price," I responded.

"Is there anything we can help you with?" Antonio asked. "My money shouldn't be held up by someone snooping around my place."

"Our goal is to get rid of the problems. Gigi and I are working on it," I explained.

Antonio checked up. "How are you doing outside of the issues at hand?"

"Taking it one day at a time."

"They tell you marriage and cartel life don't mix. My wife and I have been through everything you could think of. The most critical thing is to make sure your wife is your partner, first and foremost," Antonio said.

I stood, and I extended a hand to Antonio.

He shook it. "We'll be in touch."

"Sabrina and Janice will have extra security until things die down," Carlo said.

"I wouldn't expect anything less. I'll tell my men," I replied.

Chapter 12

Gigi

"Mrs. Bresciani."

I turned to see Ralfie holding a phone.

I panicked. "What's wrong? Is it Axel? My son?"

Ralfie held out the phone to me. "It's Oliver, ma'am."

I took the phone. "Hello?"

Oliver grumbled, "We have a problem."

My senses went on alert and I slipped into mob Boss mode. "Where?"

"My club."

"I'm on my way." I ended the call.

"Do you need me to call Mr. Bresciani?" Ralfie asked.

My nostrils twitched. "No. He has enough to deal with handling Turin's recovery."

Ralfie escorted me back to the limo, and we headed into the city. I nibbled on my nails to control my nerves. Hugo had our cars tracked, and that's how we'd gotten hit on so many times. Oliver was one of our top men in our organization. He was arrogant and hated to lose money, so had no choice but to see him.

"You two stay behind me," I told my other soldiers as Ralfie opened my door.

The club was quiet as they prepared for opening time later tonight. I knocked on Oliver's door and it was yanked open by an angry-looking girl who bumped into me on her way out.

"I was standing here," I remarked.

She poked her chest out like she was ready to fight. "Please. He'll sleep with you and leave you like he does all the girls."

"I don't work here, sweetheart."

"You're not his type, anyway," she huffed.

"Tiffany, get back to the bar," Oliver barked.

I watched her stomp off before entering the office and closing the door. "I told you about sleeping with the women here."

He hunched his shoulders. "Habit I can't break."

"What did you call me about?"

"This." He clicked the remote in his hand and the TV showed Dario and Ginerva sitting in a booth.

I stumbled back. "They're bold."

"Extremely. My product was taken last night."

I looked at Oliver. "How did they get in here?"

"Killed a few of my men and left through the side exit." Oliver pointed at the screen.

"How much was taken?"

"At least two bags."

I rubbed my forehead. "Shit."

"The guns were stripped of their serial numbers."

"That was a sale we'd planned to go down at the end of the month with the Irish mafia."

"The Irish aren't happy. They want their product now."

I paced in front of his desk. "We need to buy some time."

Oliver sighed. "I've put them off for now, but I don't like losing money, Gigi."

I whipped around to look at him. "You won't."

"Axel needs to know."

"He will."

Oliver motioned at the screen. "And them?"

"I plan on making contact soon."

"I heard Mendoza's with them."

"He wants our territory."

"I have too much tied in with the Carrington's. I don't plan on Hugo taking a cut of my percentage."

"He'll be dead soon."

"And the Irish boys? What do I do about holding them off?"

I opened the door to leave. "Give me some time to think, but for now, we move some things around and take from the warehouse in Queens."

* * *

When I got home, Axel surprised me with a date. I wore my best dress, curled my hair, and put on some light makeup. Axel was so taken with my look, he was ready to get me undressed again.

"What did you do to the doctor?" Turin's getting shot had scared me, and I was glad he was on the mend.

"I paid Dr. Nathaniel and Heather to keep quiet," Axel responded, knocking back the rest of his vodka.

He looked more like his old self tonight in a black suit, with his shirt partially open, showing his muscular chest.

The restaurant outside the city was heavily guarded, inside and out.

I took a sip from my water glass. "Any idea if he'll talk?"

Axel reached across the table for my hand. "He's not stupid. Neither is the nurse."

"Oliver called me earlier today."

Axel motioned for the server to refill his glass. "How did you handle it?"

"Ginerva and Dario stole two bags of guns that were reserved for the Irish."

"Do you need me to handle anything?" He caressed my palm.

"Not yet. How is Turin doing?"

"He's up on his feet. I told him to stay with us for a few more days."

"What did Antonio talk with you about?"

"Hugo tried to contact him to make a deal without us."

"Antonio doesn't like people who come in from the outside."

Axel reached in his pocket and pulled out his wallet, putting cash on top of the check. "Hugo tried to play it off like we agreed to give up some areas."

I put my dessert in the to-go box. "I think it's time I contacted Ginerva, then you get the Irish to show up."

Axel opened the back door for me, escorting me out of the restaurant. I pressed my hand on his chest and kissed him on the lips. When we reached the limo, he held the door then climbed in after me.

Ralfie started the engine and pulled away from the restaurant into traffic. I grabbed Axel's hand and leaned my head against his shoulder. His hand traveled to the top of my knee, and I listened to his heartbeat.

My phone rang, and I grabbed it from my purse.

"Mrs. Carrington, I see why all the men in your life grovel at your feet."

"Hugo...Hugo Mendoza?" My gaze flew to Axel.

"I know we got off on the wrong foot, but I think we can establish a friendship."

"You tried to have my husband and me killed."

"Igor was my favorite nephew."

"Igor tried to kill me."

"A little mistake."

"My husband is going to kill you."

"Dario said you were fiery. I like that in a woman."

"Never use Dario's and my name in the same sentence."

"I believe he killed your mother and father, correct?"

"I want my guns back."

"I want Chicago and New York."

"Return my property, and I'll think about letting you live."

He laughed. "Threats. My, my. Dario was right. I may have to taste you before I kill you."

Axel snatched the phone out of my hand. "Mendoza, you're messing with the wrong person."

"Axel, I suggest you buckle up tight. A bigger explosion could always happen." Hugo dropped the call.

Axel handed me my phone as we arrived home. We stepped into the house to find Turin sitting at the kitchen island talking with Ebony, while the nanny held Gaspare.

"Take him upstairs," Axel demanded.

"Axel, calm down."

"Gigi, not now." Axel paced back and forth.

"What's going on?" Turin asked.

Axel smacked his hand against the wall, and Gaspare started to cry.

"You're scaring him." I picked up my son and kissed him on the cheek.

"Hugo sent a message," Axel growled.

I glared at Axel. "Can you put him to bed?" I asked the nanny.

"Yes, of course," she answered.

"Ebony, you can go for the night," I informed her with a smile, watching as she removed her apron and left the kitchen.

"No more bullshitting. We need to find them now," Axel muttered.

I followed behind him to his office with Turin. "I can contact Ginerva tomorrow."

Axel opened his door and reached for the telephone. "I'll be ready," Turin responded.

"I have an idea, but you won't like it," I said.

"Then it's a no." Axel took a seat in his chair.

"Axel, hear me out." I took the phone out of his hand and hung it up.

Turin agreed with me. "She can get to Ginerva, which will lead us to Dario."

I bit my lip. "Antonio will back us up, so... what if I confess to Igor's death?"

Axel jumped out of his seat. "*What?*"

I pushed him down and sat in his lap, caressing his cheek. "I'll confess to Raymond and Soren."

"No." Axel was resolute.

"Gigi, that only creates more problems," Turin pointed out.

"What if we ensure Ginerva *and* Hugo attend?" I suggested.

Axel murmured. "You mean, kidnap Ginerva?"

"With Ginerva gone, Dario will have no choice but to raise his head," I reasoned.

"Could work," Turin agreed.

I had another idea as backup. "I could pretend I want Dario back."

"Dario won't fall for that," Axel snapped.

"He will if I confess to Igor's death and make Hugo a deal. Soren wants money. We fake it and have each of them turn on the other."

"It won't work."

"Axel, you said to think more like an Enforcer instead of a husband. This is the perfect opportunity. We're doing it my way."

I knew once Turin left and Gaspare was asleep, Axel would punish me for my direct challenge.

* * *

The bedroom door slammed. I stood in place, not reacting. His breath tickled the back of my neck as he wrapped his hand around my hair and yanked. I gasped as his chest met my back.

"Put your palms out." Slowly, his hands moved downward, skimming either side of my body to my thighs.

"Axel."

"Now!" He caressed the skin of my thigh, and the gentle massage sent currents of desire through my body.

"Yes, sir."

Axel's fingers burned into my tingling skin as I placed my palms on top of the dresser. He kicked my legs apart and pressed his lips to my shoulder before tracing the curve of my neck. "Do you know who the fuck I am?"

I heard the clink of his belt buckle. He slipped a hand to the front of my dress and yanked the straps down to expose my breasts. He gripped them and flicked my nipples.

"You're m-my husband," I moaned as I pushed my ass into him.

Axel turned and lifted me onto the dresser. He dipped his head and sucked on my neck while he pinched my nipple.

I tossed my head back and gripped the back of his head, pushing my chest forward. "Yes, please."

His eyes were fathomless, an abyss of pleasure. "If you ever talk to me like that again—"

I pushed him off me and jumped down. "What are you going to do, Axel?"

His frown cleared at my challenge, and he pushed me up against the wall. I wrapped my legs around his waist, and we moaned as he slid his hard length inside me.

"God! I can't go without you again," he groaned.

"Baby!"

His hand circled my throat. "I can't live without you, Gigi."

"Fuck me harder." I pleaded.

Axel brushed his lips against mine. "God, I love this tight pussy. Fucking kills me every time."

I swallowed my cry and gripped his shoulders as he rutted me further up the wall. "Axel, oh God. You can't hold me... like... fuck!" I cried out as he pulled out and spun to face the wall. He thrust back inside me, pumping in and out. "Oh, God. Don't stop!"

"Shush," he grunted. "You'll wake Gaspare."

I smacked my hand on the wall. "I can't help...Axel!"

Axel took my mouth with a savage intensity. I breathed in a deep. Soul-yearning tremor when his hardness stroked against my spot and my thighs flooded with my arousal.

He pulled out, and I glared at him over my shoulder.

"Kneel on the floor."

"Are you sure you can handle me?" I wrapped my hand around his dick.

He bent down and pressed a kiss on my lips. "More than capable of handling you."

Hypnotized by the sexiness of his girth, I took him in my mouth and fixed my eyes on his. I breathed through my nose and rubbed his balls as he whispered encouragement in a low, silky voice. I extended my tongue and relaxed my throat as he guided me up and down on his dick.

"Suck it just like that, baby," he grunted.

I bobbed my head up and down until his hand grew tight around my hair and I knew he was about to explode.

I pulled back and spat on his tip, twisting my hand up and down and watching his head fall back.

He slowly fucked my face, and I took him all the way down to his pubic bone.

"Fuck! Gigi."

I pushed a finger into my pussy as he released in my mouth. I closed my eyes as I thought of his dick pounding me and came in a rush.

Afterward, we showered and curled up in bed.

In the middle of the night, Gaspare cried, and I left the bed with a little fight from Axel. I slipped on my robe, went to his room, and lifted him from his crib.

"You couldn't sleep?" I walked around the room cradled him in my arms.

He yawned and smiled.

"My biggest blessing."

Gaspare reached for my hand and tried to put it in his mouth.

"Such a good boy."

Axel stood at the door. "He's going to get spoiled."

"Like his daddy."

Axel took Gaspare and rubbed his back. "Buddy, you need to sleep, so Mommy can get what she needs."

I stood and watched him put Gaspare back in his crib. "What do I need?" I gnawed on my top lip.

Axel hooked an arm around my waist. "Sleep, so you're ready to take on the Mendoza Cartel."

"Is this you finally understanding I need an Enforcer *and* a husband?"

"Yes." Axel kissed me. "Forgive me."

I nodded. "Always."

Chapter 13

Axel

The hot water from the shower pelted me, easing muscles that were numb from working out. I'd been avoiding extra appointments with a physical therapist and doing my own thing, keeping Gigi out of the loop. I'd always been the one to handle the storm when anything came our way, but now I needed to rely more and more on her. Seemed the only way to get my body back to a hundred percent was to follow doctor's orders and stick to my routine.

Sleep was the only time I had bursts of memory of the explosion. Otherwise, it didn't cross my mind because Gaspare and Gigi kept me busy throughout the day.

I turned off the shower, picked up the towel, and wrapped it around my waist. Drying my hair with another one, I left the bathroom and got dressed to prepare for my doctor's visit. Downstairs, Gigi was feeding Gaspare on the sofa with a cartoon of a pig on in the background.

She smiled as she saw me. "Where are you off to so early?"

"To meet with Oliver," I lied.

"Why didn't you tell me last night?"

I bent and kissed her on the lips before kissing Gaspare's forehead. "Forgot. I won't be gone long."

"Hey." Gigi grabbed my wrist as I turned to leave. "Is everything okay with us?"

"Yeah."

She smiled and released my wrist.

* * *

Ralfie pulled up to the hospital and since it would be a brief visit, I asked him to wait outside. Soon as I checked in, the nurse took me Doctor Nathaniel's office. He was on the phone as I entered and obviously harbored anxiety from my previous visit as he stiffened in his chair. He told whoever he was talking to on the phone to call back.

"What are you doing here?"

I held up my hands. "I come in peace. I need to get a checkup."

"Checkup?"

"For me."

"But—"

I waved my hand in his face. "Only you can do it, so cancel whatever appointments you have for the next hour or two."

"Mr. Bresciani, it doesn't work like that at this hospital."

"As far as what works, we had a talk about what's in store for your family, and you're the only one who knows my lifestyle."

"Not by choice."

"You're being paid handsomely."

"Money isn't the reason."

"The nurse comes by, but I wanted to get your opinion."

"On what?"

"If I'm ever going to be me again."

"I'm not a therapist."

"And I don't need you to be, but sometimes I feel like I lost my body in the coma."

"Unfortunately, that's normal. Give yourself time to heal."

"My work lacks vacation time."

He stood and grabbed his equipment. "Come with me and I'll do some follow-up testing if that will make you feel better."

"It will."

* * *

I listened to Gigi talk about her day and plans for Gaspare.

"I'll call you later. Be safe." I ended our call.

"She good?" Turin asked.

I told Turin to stay home, but he was stubborn, like me. "No."

"What happened?"

"She's stressed because we didn't wait the full six weeks."

"Damn. Did the doctor say something?"

I rubbed a hand over my face. "She's worried if we don't use protection, she'll end up pregnant again."

"Man, you sure didn't wait," Turin joked.

"I could never do that with her." I grinned.

"Keep your focus." Turin lifted his gun.

I tapped on the window as I strolled to the shipyard to meet Hugo. A few cars arrived with backup from Antonio, and I lifted my chin in recognition. Onyx led the way through the door, where Hugo was sitting at a table surrounded by his men.

He clasped his hands together and stared at me, his face emotionless. I clenched my jaw. I couldn't kill until we had what we needed.

"My deal is final, no negotiations," Hugo stated.

"Deal with Dario or the Irish mafia?" I asked.

"All of the above. You decided your terms, and I have mine." He reached into his pocket and grabbed a cigarette and lighter.

"The terms my wife gave Igor in Chicago are still on the table, as is letting you live."

Anger heated his face. "Threats only get you more pain, and I would say you've been through enough."

"Hugo, we've made it clear that if you go against us, you become the bigger threat we have to eliminate."

Hugo pulled on the cigarette and put it out on the table. "The Irish received a package from Dario. You will have no choice but to send your pretty little wife to prison unless I receive the money as compensation for her killing my nephew."

I reached for my gun and every soldier in the room raised their weapons.

Hugo frowned and stood. "You're not the only one prepared to die."

"Keep my wife out of this."

The door opened and heels clicked against the floor. I knew only one person who discover something I wanted to keep secret.

Gigi stood next to me and dropped her purse on the

table. "Hugo, I suggest you move that gun away from my husband's face."

"Is this bad cop, good cop?"

I scoffed and rose from the chair.

Gigi placed a hand on my shoulder to stop me. "Hugo, I killed your nephew, and I don't regret it, so I suggest you listen carefully."

"Bitch!" he snarled and lunged at her.

I pushed her behind me and charged at him, but Ralfie and his guard got between us.

"Axel, I'm fine," Gigi said.

"Detective Soren will hear about this," Hugo threatened.

"You can get whoever you want. We will never give you territory," Gigi said calmly.

"The Irish deal will give me more power. I can take New York. Fuck the De Lucas," Hugo spat, jerking out of Onyx's hold.

"I won't forget the ambush you set up," I warned him.

Hugo ignored me and walked out of the room.

Gigi whipped to face me with a glare. She planted on her hips on her hips and tapped her foot.

"Leave us," I instructed our men.

"You lied to me," she accused as soon as we were alone.

"It was easier to make you believe I came to visit Oliver."

"So you met with Hugo behind my back?"

"I did."

"And the doctor's visit?"

"How did you—"

"The nurse called and said your tests came back clear."

I didn't want her thinking I was trying to hinder her from being the person she was born to be. "I apologize."

Gigi walked up to me and looped her arms around my neck. "I forgive you, but we don't keep secrets. Ever."

I raised her chin. "That means we're locked in for life."

"Locked in for life, and I want you to be honest about everything you're dealing with when it comes to your health. I'm still pissed that we didn't wait my six weeks."

I grinned, and she smacked me on the chest.

Gigi and I looked toward the door as Turin honked the car horn, his signal that he was ready to go. I reached for her hand and we walked out to a surprise appearance from Detectives Soren and Raymond.

"Mr. and Mrs. Bresciani! Is there a reason you're at an abandoned shipyard?" Soren asked.

I opened the car door and helped Gigi get in before sliding in next to her. "It's a free country, Detective."

Detective Soren kept his hand on his phone as Raymond glanced around the building.

"Anything else?" I asked politely.

"We'll be seeing you very soon."

"Unless we see you first, Detective."

* * *

I filled Gigi in on the plan to get Ginerva, and the location of the motel.

"Are you sure you want to go through with this?" I asked her.

"Yes," Gigi immediately replied.

"There's no turning back after this," I said, searching her eyes.

Gigi confirmed, "I have no remorse."

"Okay, here are the schematics for the location where we believe she's staying with Dario."

"Are you going in with them?" Gigi asked.

"Yeah, and if Dario is there, we take him."

"I know you want his blood, but don't kill him."

"I promised I would keep him for you."

"I wish you didn't have to go." She rubbed her palm over my chest.

I leaned in and pecked her on the lips.

Gigi shoved the pictures of Dario away and picked up the picture of Ginerva eating lunch alone.

"Better to make sure they pick up the right girl. It's a motel, so anything could go wrong."

Gigi begged, "Just come home safe."

"My only thought is you and our son." I rubbed her stomach.

Gigi moved my hand off her stomach. "No more of that, either."

"Why? We've already made the leap."

"Leap? That's what you call us having sex?"

I held in my laugh and kissed the back of her hand before moving off the bed. I grabbed my holster, gun, jacket, and the knife I liked to use when I chased someone down. "We can talk about that when I get back."

Gigi followed me downstairs and watched me from the front door of the house as Turin started the car and I climbed into the passenger seat.

Turin announced. "Ready?"

"For kidnapping? Always."

Turin followed behind Onyx, and we headed for the motel. The ride passed quickly, and it was just past 9 PM when we pulled up outside. Turin looked left and right as we approached the building, to ensure no one saw us while walked ahead of us.

We took the elevator to the fifth floor. As we stopped out, a gunshot rang out, and a bullet whizzed past us.

"Shit!"

I raised my gun as her motel door opened, and Ginerva poked her head out.

"Get down!" Her guard yelled as I sent shots back at him and took cover around the corner. Turin was on the opposite side with Onyx.

"What is going on?" Ginerva screamed.

"Dario's not here. We need to run!" the guard shouted.

Ginerva panicked. "I don't have my things."

"Leave them!" he yelled.

I peeked from behind the wall as he grabbed and started for the exit.

"Don't move!" I yelled, levelling my weapon at the guard.

He raised his gun, and I fired off two shots. Ginerva screamed and dropped to the floor as his body fell in the exit door. I jogged over and kicked the gun away from him before checking for a pulse.

"Get her and check the room," I instructed Onyx.

"No! Help me!"

Onyx covered her mouth, carrying her down the stairs and through the back exit to the alley. Turin entered the room with me while Ralfie got rid of the guard's body.

I scanned the room. Clothes, shoes and newspapers were strewn around, along with empty takeout cartons. Dario must have felt closed in for him to put her up in such a dingy place.

Turin picked up her purse, removed her phone, and

scrolled through the unknown numbers. He dialed the one number that appeared repeatedly.

"Ginerva, what the fuck you doing calling me?"

Turin put the phone on speaker. "This isn't Ginerva."

Dario chuckled. "I guess it was time you found her."

I said, "Maybe you should come and meet us."

"She won't talk."

"Are you sure about that?"

"Does Gigi miss me? It's been a while since we've talked."

"She's busy being a wife and mother."

The phone went silent.

"You picked up my seconds. I might take her back once I kill you," Dario taunted me.

I took the phone out of Turin's hand. "You fucked up. You should've made sure I died in the explosion."

"Next time, I'll do it myself."

"Hugo can't save you."

"I have other resources. Don't underestimate me," he growled.

"I'd suggest you get your will in order because it's time to end this."

"Make sure you're ready because I don't plan on going down easy," he snapped, then hung up.

We stepped out of the room as Ralfie approached. "From the motel security," he said, holding up the tapes.

"Did you have problems getting them?"

He grinned. "Security's asleep."

I took the tapes, and we drove to the warehouse to destroy them and my clothes. Ginerva tried to bite Ralfie and Onyx as they took her to a secure room and tied her to a chair. I gave orders to the team to keep her locked without water and food until I said so.

"Dario's going to kill you!" she screamed.

I shut the warehouse door behind me and went to the car to wait for Turin.

A few minutes passed before Turin slid into the passenger seat. "She's asleep."

"What did you give her?"

"Something to keep her knocked out for a few hours."

"Good. I want Gigi to be here when we get answers. She needs this closure."

We backed out of the dirt road and headed to my place to regroup. I needed to shower and climb into bed with my wife.

I gripped the steering wheel in anticipation. Dario was the reason my parents weren't here anymore. Death would be too easy for him, so I intended to make it painful.

"What are you thinking about?"

"How much I'll enjoy ending everybody who has destroyed something in my life."

The thought of Gigi never feeling safe would end soon, our dark place wouldn't last much longer. Ginerva would talk or not, but she'd sealed her fate with her betrayal.

Chapter 14

Axel

The smell of piss and acid filled the air from the awful cologne Connor Murphy continued to drown himself in every time we met. He was one of those guys who thought people fell at their feet.

I'd avoided most of the meetings with the Murphy Cartel and let Turin handle them back in Italy. Hugo trying to partner with the Irish and putting the police on our tails made me more testy than usual.

Gigi stood beside me. I hadn't wanted her here, but with everything going on, I preferred to keep her close.

"Axel, the last time we met, you had a gun in my face," Connor said with a smirk.

I let him have his little remark. I knew it was a jab to get me riled up. I tipped my head at him. "Connor."

He grinned. "I hear my guns are gone."

"And I hear you're trying to set a deal up with Hugo Mendoza."

He shrugged. "Business."

"Mr. Murphy, I'm Gigi Bresciani, the Boss of

Carrington Cartel and Axel's wife." She extended her hand to him.

I pulled it back, and Connor chuckled.

"I see you don't let stray animals go to waste by choosing Axel of all people," Connor remarked.

I drew Gigi close. "I'm the lucky one."

"We're here because you went behind our backs to deal with the Mendoza Cartel. Are you aware that Hugo Mendoza and Dario Ramini are trying to cut us out on the sale?" Gigi asked.

"At the moment, all I care about are my guns. We've been in business for years, but we want to make New York one of our bigger distribution hubs," Connor explained.

"That can't happen, Mr. Murphy, because De Luca and I have this territory, and we're not selling." Gigi glared at him.

He didn't seem happy at her statement. "Mendoza gave me better numbers. Dario brought the opportunity to me, and I agreed."

"He stole your guns," I said.

"To sell back to you at a higher rate," Gigi added.

Connor whispered to his partners, Cillian and Fionn, and they all nodded. "How will you make this worth our time if we don't go with Hugo?"

Gigi and I made eye contact. "We are willing to give you a lower rate on future sales and cut ties with any other Ireland deals. We'll only deal with you from now on."

Connor didn't wait to confirm with his men before he held his hand out. "I like the sound of that. You know we want you gone from our territory as soon as possible."

Laurent had land in Ireland and years of deals set in

place. It would take a little time to get everything transferred over while we handled Hugo and Dario.

"We need a little time. The Carringtons have a long history in Ireland," I answered.

"You have one week," Connor countered and left with his men.

Oliver jumped up in irritation. "What the fuck just happened?"

"Business, Oliver," Gigi responded.

"That leaves us out of pocket. No offense, Axel, but leaving Ireland deals off the table will cost us."

"Oliver, we know what we're doing," Gigi replied.

"Losing Ireland will cost us, but we need to eliminate Hugo and Dario for good," I explained.

Not in the mood for more questions, I grabbed Gigi's hand and escorted her from the building. I helped Gigi into the car, and as I was about to climb in, my skin prickled with a premonition. Tires screeched as a car roared past, a gun leveled at us through the passenger window.

I pulled my weapon and fired at the gunman. The rest of our men returned fire, and the car screeched off with the shooter slumped in the seat, riddled with bullets. I yanked the car door open and released a breath when I saw Gigi had taken cover. I pulled her to me and checked her over for any wounds.

"Hey, you're safe. I'm here," I whispered in her ear, kissing her forehead and cheek.

Gigi tugged my head down and her lips crashed into mine.

My gun automatically went up as Turin climbed in the car.

He grinned and raised his hands in the air when he

saw my weapon. "It's just me. You good, Gigi?"

"I'm fine, Turin. Anyone hit?"

"They're fine. The shooter was focused on you."

I climbed out of the car and helped Gigi to stand. "Did anybody get their license?"

The block was empty considering it was afternoon in the New York business district. Someone knew we had a meeting today.

"No, but what are the odds Connor and Hugo are behind an ambush?"

I rubbed my chin in thought. "Connor's not dumb. We just handed him at least a hundred million by pulling out of Ireland. He won't shed blood."

"Then it's Dario and Hugo."

"I agree with Turin. Any news on Dario?" Gigi questioned.

"We got Ginerva," Turin said.

"*What?*"

"I wanted to wait and tell you, but I got home late," I explained.

"You had her and didn't tell me?"

"Now's not the time to argue. We can talk when we get home."

Another car arrived, and I helped Gigi inside. I sat beside her as Ralfie removed our things from the limo.

"I'll meet you later," Turin said, and went to speak with Onyx.

We hurried to leave the scene before the police arrived. Gigi ignored me and stared out of the window. I hadn't deliberately held anything back from her; it was just late when I made it home and my only thought had been of being with her and my son. Her mood would improve once I got her alone.

"I want to take you somewhere," I murmured.

"We can't."

"We haven't had a proper honeymoon or been alone together."

"Right now is not the time, Axel."

"Gigi, I didn't keep the news about Ginerva from you on purpose."

She turned to face me. "I believe you."

I rubbed her thigh. "The Connor deal was a good decision."

"Oliver thinks it was stupid."

"Oliver's opinion doesn't matter. He'll never understand how you run the cartel."

"He's in a position where we need his support."

"His support, but not his opinions."

Gigi's eyes met mine. "I've been thinking of stepping back and focusing on our son more."

"You worked hard as the Don of the cartel."

She rubbed my knuckles. "Did Ginerva say anything?"

"Not yet. I wanted to keep her under wraps until you could get to her."

She smiled. "You're always thinking about me."

"You're my wife."

Gigi reached for the partition button and rolled it up as she ran her fingers through my hair. "I want to do something for you."

"What do you have in mind?"

"Something that will make us both very happy," she said, grinding against my hard length.

"So you're no longer worried about me using protection and getting pregnant?"

"Still worried, but maybe you could—"

I slowly drew my tongue across her bottom lip, keeping my eyes on hers as I sucked it into my mouth. "No pulling out."

She nibbled on my neck, and I moaned when she reached down to grab my stiff dick. Cool air hit me as she lowered my zipper, and I closed my eyes as she ran the tip of her tongue over my crown. My hips jerked, and I grabbed the back of her head in a haze. The way she moved her mouth up and down should be against the law. I knew when we first got together that she was inexperienced, but time and practice had made her a pro at pleasing me. My wife knew how to get me to the brink and keep me satisfied, over and over again. She was the only woman who could turn me on and piss me off in equal measure, and I wanted to fuck her until we passed out.

The second the car pulled up at the house, I pulled her out and carried her up the stairs to our bedroom. I stripped us of our clothes, and Gigi dropped to her knees before I could even give her sweet pussy a kiss.

"Damn it, Gigi." My head fell back, and I pictured our first time making love.

My desire for my wife echoed in my mind all day, every day, and seeing her body after giving birth to our baby only made me hotter for her.

Her eyes closed, and she rubbed across my stomach. A wave of emotions swept over me when she touched me. I needed to be buried deep inside her to get my thoughts together. During these vulnerable moments, my Italian blood came to the forefront.

"*Amore mio!* Get up here."

Gigi released me with a pop and stroked me with her hand before straddling me. With her eyes fixed on mine, she lined me up with her core and slowly took me inside her tight heat.

"I...oh, God," she cooed.

"Feels like heaven."

I didn't want to end our play too early, so I pulled out of her and switched position, delving my tongue into her sweet honey. Her juices created a wet spot on the bed and drove me crazy every time.

I eased a finger inside her, watching as she wriggled under my hold. Her movements anticipated mine, and she gripped my shoulders as my tongue moved in and out. Her back arched off the bed, and I planted my hand on her stomach to keep her down while I feasted on her. I kissed her inner thigh, biting and nibbling as I moved my tongue down her leg and kissed her toes.

Our problems melted away as we connected on a deeper level.

A bite to her inner thigh caused her to shiver under my grip and caused one of my favorite things to happen.

I growled as she squirted in my face, and I crawled up the bed like a lion. I hovered over her body and thrust back into her core, planted my hands on either side of her as I drove deep and circled my hips.

"Shit! I'm going to come," she gasped.

"Fuck! Look at me, baby. You take my dick so well. All I want is you."

"Oh...yes! Yes!"

I nutted as soon as she came and fell on top of her, out of breath. I pulled Gigi into my arms and kissed her on the forehead and lips.

Gigi purred. "That was unexpected."

Taking a piece of her hair, I twisted it. "It was necessary to release the stress."

She looked up at me and pushed her leg over my hip. "Everything good with you ?" she asked, caressing my cheek.

"Never been more focused than now." I was ready to go out on a killing spree, but I needed to make sure my family was happy and safe.

I went to get out of bed, but she climbed on top of me. The covers fell down, and my eyes went to her full breasts. I took one in my mouth and she moaned.

She gently cupped the back of my head. "We need to eat and see Gaspare first."

I released her breast and nodded. "I missed him."

Gigi rose from the bed and grabbed her robe. "Me, too. Ebony probably has lunch ready."

I watched her go into the drawer and grab fresh panties and a bra.

"Come shower with me."

"You go ahead. I need to check on things."

"Don't be too long." Gigi winked and headed for the bathroom, leaving the door open as she showered.

I scrolled to Turin's message thread to see if there were any updates on Ginerva.

Me: *How is she?*

Turin: *She woke up, and we offered her food, but she refused to eat.*

Me: *She probably thinks Dario will save her.*

Turin: *I had her put back to sleep.*

Me: *Good. We'll keep her on ice for another day to see if he makes contact.*

I tossed the phone on the bed and strolled into the bathroom. I stood at the counter and watched Gigi in the shower as she hummed while washing her hair. Laurent put me in this life. All I'd cared about was revenge and making Laurent and my parents proud. To have Gigi and my son was a blessing I never thought possible. No woman would ever compare to her.

I pushed off the counter and nudged the door open.

She looked over her shoulder and smiled. "Everything okay?"

"Everything is fine." I stepped inside and picked up the sponge and bodywash to wash her shoulders and back. I kissed her neck, and she reached behind her to pull me close.

"I love you, Axel, and I know you're doing what's best for our family."

"I love you more, Gigi."

Much later, we left the bathroom to find our son.

Gaspare sat in the nanny's arms playing with his toy bear, but as soon as Gigi and I came into the room and he saw us, he smiled and clapped his hands for us to pick him up. Gigi took him and kissed all over his face. I sat down, smiling as I watched them interact. He slobbered all over her face as she nuzzled their noses together.

"You want to see Daddy?" Gigi asked, smiling as he replied in his own baby talk.

"Baby, you spoil him."

"You spoiled me." She passed him to me and I kissed his cheek and smelled his hair.

"Nothing about him looks like me," Gigi complained.

Gigi was right. He looked just like me as a baby. "The next one will come out looking more like you." I winked at her.

Her lips twitched. "Next one? I think that's a no-go, buddy."

The nanny laughed and stood to leave the room as I sat back on the couch.

"One, maybe two more," Gigi conceded. "In a few years."

Gaspare played in my arms while she explained how we needed to wait before we had another baby.

"When are we going to see Ginerva?" she suddenly asked.

"Tomorrow. She refused to talk, so we need to let her sit."

"I want to talk to her."

"You will. Give her time to realize that Dario can't save her."

"How did she seem when you caught her?"

"He'd put her up in a shabby motel on the outskirts of Queens."

"Dario's running scared." Gigi picked up Gaspare's baby bib and wiped the slobber off his lips and chin. She grabbed the bottle off the floor and handed it to me to feed him.

At moments like this, I realized how my son would have me at his beck and call for the rest of his life. "He doesn't seem to care that we took her. All he talked about was you."

She jerked back at my words. "Me? He's lost his mind."

"Once Connor lets Hugo know the deal, Dario will try to run. So be ready."

"He can't hurt me anymore."

I reached around and pulled her to my side. She picked up the remote and turned on the TV. We watched a movie for the rest of the day and had dinner as a family. It was just the three of us, and I preferred it that way.

Chapter 15

Gigi

After sleeping in, I took Gaspare for a check-up.

"Baby Gaspare is gaining weight nicely," the doctor said.

I smiled. "He's such a happy baby. I want him to stay like this forever."

She laughed. "And how is mom doing?"

I leaned against the table. "Good. Busy."

"Remember, you need to take care of yourself, too."

"Sometimes it feels like there aren't enough hours in the day."

"As a mother, I understand, but Gaspare needs you rested and healthy."

"Thanks. I promise, Doctor."

"He's all set."

I put Gaspare back in his car seat and grabbed his baby bag. I thanked the doctor again and headed to the front desk to make a follow-up appointment. Ralfie and Onyx were waiting at the car when I emerged from the building.

When Gaspare was of age, he'd have guards for the

rest of his life. Growing up in a cartel family wasn't ideal for any child, and I knew how it hurt me when I wanted to be free and explore at a young age. My mother and father had forbidden me from doing anything. Now I was a parent, I understood the stress and constant worry that someone might try to hurt my child to get back at me.

"Ralfie, take me to the mall first. I need to grab a few things for Gaspare."

"Ma'am, Mr. Bresciani wanted me to drop you right off."

"It won't take long."

Ralfie looked at Onyx. They seemed scared to defy my husband's orders.

"I will take the blame, gentleman. One hour, tops."

Ralfie drove to the mall closest to our house, which was a compromise I could handle. The drive was peaceful and didn't take more than ten minutes as Gaspare slept in the car seat. Onyx grabbed the stroller, and I took Gaspare out and picked up my purse, then walked with them behind me.

"One hour," Ralfie confirmed.

I lifted my pinky finger. "One hour, Scouts honor."

The Baby's Emperor was my favorite store to shop for my baby boy, and they had new items every week. I had some things put on hold and wanted to grab a few new trinkets. But as we made it to the entrance, I smelled a familiar cologne and wrinkled my nose in disgust.

Detectives Soren and Raymond blocked me from entering the store. "I knew we'd see each other soon."

"What can I do for you, Detective Soren?"

"How's Connor Murphy?"

"Who?"

He chuckled and his partner glared at me. "Keep up the fakeness. I like to play dumb, too."

"I have no idea what you're talking about."

"Connor Murphy is in town."

"Okay."

Detective Soren tilted his head. "An Irish cartel is in my city and you have no idea why?"

"Nope."

"Don't play games!" he hissed, gripping my arm.

Ralfie pushed him back. He stumbled and would have fallen if Raymond hadn't caught him.

"Don't touch her," Ralfie growled.

"It's fine, Ralfie," I reassured him. "Detective Soren's not crazy enough to do anything to me in public."

"I can have you arrested for assaulting an officer," he hissed, poking a finger at Ralfie's chest.

"You approached me and harassed my guards." I pointed out.

"Fuck you and your guards. I know you met with Connor Murphy."

"How many times are you going to throw accusations at me?" I sighed and shook my head. "Connor. Mendoza. Please find a hobby and leave me alone."

He tried to lunge at me, but Raymond held him back.

"You should leave, Detective. You're only making things worse for yourself."

"We'll meet again," he threatened.

"Clearly you have a vendetta against me."

"Nothing would give me more pleasure than to see you behind bars."

"How much do you make, Detective?"

"Are you bribing me? That's against the law."

I raised my hands. "Not bribing, just curious if you

make a decent living. Every time I turn around, I see your face, so that tells me being a cop pays very little. Maybe I could put in a few referrals with your superiors to get you a raise." I patted him on the arm and walked around him into the store.

Ralfie called Axel while I shopped. Axel demanded I go home when he found out about Detective Soren approached us. Being out of the house was nice, and I was not ready to go home, so the compromise was having me on FaceTime while I shopped.

The detectives followed us out of the mall, but we ditched them on the way home when we stopped to get groceries.

After I got Gaspare down with the nanny, I went out again, this time to the club to meet Connor. Oliver handled sales at his club, but I promised to personally handle the transaction so no other mistakes occurred. Oliver glared while Connor spoke with his men while, not happy we were making a deal that would cost us money.

"Mr. Murphy, we have ten crates ready. You can check them now."

Connor stopped talking and scanned the shipment in the corner. "What if we want more?"

My brow went up. "More?"

"You think we shouldn't do business with him, but Mendoza had a great offer."

"Sorry you think you have a choice in the matter, but the deal is non-negotiable."

He balled his hands into fists. "Anything can be bought." He licked his lips and leered at me.

"Take what you came for and leave, motherfucker," Oliver barked.

"Oliver, our past business is a fond memory, but you know disrespect is not tolerated," Connor warned, stepping in his face.

"Connor, step back. Oliver is right. You agreed to this deal, and you'll get your money and guns."

"Mendoza promised us New York and the distribution of guns."

"He can't promise something he doesn't even have."

"Not our problem," Cillian, Connor's brother, argued.

I blew out a breath and closed my eyes. I counted to three and opened them again. Something had changed with Connor over the past few days, and he thought he could renege on the deal. But I knew a selfish spoiled brat when I saw one because that used to be me.

I clenched my teeth. "What did he promise you?"

Connor frowned. "Who?"

"Detective Soren." Connor was far too comfortable with Hugo and Dario's deal, which meant he was in the bed with the cops as well.

"Detective Soren?" Oliver looked from me to Connor.

I raised my hand as Connor approached me. "That's what your little show is about, right?"

"I'm not an actor, sweetheart," Connor said smugly.

"Only an actor or a liar would try to swindle me and my family."

"Deals can be broken."

I got in his face. "Not without repercussions."

Connor glanced at Cillian as I moved away.

After a moment, Oliver approached me. "What are you thinking?"

I grimace. "He's playing us, and I'm pissed he thought I would let him."

"I knew we shouldn't have given him what he wanted."

"Oliver, relax. He won't be able to get far or live to tell anyone about this deal."

"He's the head of the Murphy crime family," Oliver muttered.

I knew exactly who and what Connor Murphy was and the people behind him.

Connor stood over the crates of guns. He bent to pick one up, and Oliver reached for his weapon.

I motioned for him to wait. "Connor, I don't have all day."

He dropped the gun back in the crate and turned to face me.

"If we take the deal, we want exclusive sale on drugs into Spain and Italy."

"Are you crazy or high?"

"Plus the crate, and you out of Ireland. I thought you understood this business. Usually, men make concessions in these types of situations."

"I have a better offer. You can leave."

"Leave?"

"Yes. Leave with nothing." I waved a hand in the air.

Oliver looked shocked at my words.

Connor's eyes narrowed. "We aren't leaving without our merchandise."

"The deal is no longer yours to take. As of one minute ago, I refused to pull out of Ireland or give you the order of guns. The money will be returned to you in one hour. Have a nice flight back to Ireland, gentleman."

"Bitch! You can't cut us out!" Connor snarled. "Mendoza was right about you."

"Good! Because I can be a lot of things, but a whining

bitch is not one of them. I gave you the opportunity, and you dismissed it, so now I'm done playing nice with you assholes."

Connor reached for his gun. Ralfie and Oliver pulled their weapons.

"Neither of you will walk out of here alive," I announced.

"Fuck you!" Cillian barked.

"Detective Soren must have given you a deal to come here and betray us. Cillian, are you ready to die or go to jail for Connor?" I asked.

I knew Cillian would be loyal to his brother, but even he knew Connor was being stupid by not taking my warning.

"Shut up!" Connor shouted.

"Leave while you still can, and I'll consider not having your heads blown off on the way home."

Connor tried to negotiate. "I want what we came for."

"Sorry, the deal is off the table."

He glanced at Oliver for help.

"Oliver doesn't make deals. I run this family."

Connor lowered his gun. He could see I wouldn't bulge and left while he still could. My shoulders slumped in relief that no blood had been shed. His ego had taken a blow at the expense of a woman.

* * *

We finished at the club with Oliver and added extra security as a precaution. Then I had Ralfie take me to Axel at the warehouse. Hugo was more pissed off than usual as he paced in front of his car on the phone.

162

I approached Axel and kissed him on the lips. "Are you good?"

"You pulled the deal with Connor," he stated.

"He tried to play us. I think Soren was behind it."

Axel grinned. "Nice move."

"You think I did the right thing?"

"I would have done the same. He's too eager. He became unhinged when his father put him in charge."

"I'm glad."

"Did anyone follow you?"

"No. Ralfie took the side streets."

"Hugo looks unhappy."

"How long have you been here?"

"About thirty minutes."

"Is Ginerva awake?"

"I tried to get her to eat, but she refused again."

"I'm going to go see her."

"Take someone with you."

"I will." I stood on my tiptoes and kissed him on the lips.

I walked through the warehouse and down the hall to the room where they were keeping Ginerva. Ralfie opened the door and scanned the room before I stepped around him and saw a thinner Ginerva lying on the bed in the fetal position.

"Ginerva."

She didn't move.

"Ginerva." I kicked the bed.

She mumbled under her breath and slowly turned over, blinking from the small light in the room. She still wore the cami shorts and top from the night they took her. I barely recognized my friend with her hair matted and her arms chained to the bed.

"Ginerva, we need to talk."

"Gigi."

"Wake up."

Her eyes fully aligned with mine and she snarled, "Let me out of here!"

She tried to get loose, and I stood back and watched her.

I'd been looking for her for months. I'd dropped everything and pooled my resources into finding her. To discover that she'd been playing me all along broke my heart. I'd fooled myself into believing that Dario had threatened her, but now I knew that wasn't true. I was her enemy. She hated me and wanted me dead. Our friendship was built on lies. All the times we'd stayed talking on the phone and sharing our secrets meant nothing.

"I thought it was a dream when I saw you that day in the mall," I said softly.

"Let me out of here."

"I called your name."

"Are you going to let me go?"

"Why did you run?"

"Dario is looking for me."

"Dario?"

"He's going to find me and kill all of you."

"What happened to you, Ginerva? I don't get it."

"Kidnapping me? Dario is right about you."

"Do you hear yourself?"

"Dario loves me!"

"He's brainwashed you."

"He loves me, and you're jealous."

"I'm married. You were supposed to be married. We planned play dates with our kids."

Her laugh was evil. "Dario never wanted you. He belonged to me and only me."

"What about your parents and family?"

Remorse flickered across her face. "My family has nothing to do with Dario and me."

"I'm sorry, Ginerva. There's no coming back from what you've done."

"He's not the only one who hates you!"

I turned my back on her and walked out. Too much anger lived in her heart, and it made me question our entire lives together. My mind raced at how Dario had manipulated everyone around him to do his bidding.

I reached the front of the warehouse and saw one of our guards holding a gun to Hugo's head. His men had their weapons raised, ready for a shootout. The rooms had no sound because of what went on here and I hadn't heard a peep from Ralfie that anything went down.

I rushed to Axel and hugged him tight. "What happened?"

Axel placed a hand around my waist. "Hugo thought he could call for backup."

"I still have the evidence on your wife," Hugo shouted, banging his palm on the table.

I moved toward him, but Axel held me back. "Evidence or not, you will never walk out of here alive."

"My team is aware I'm here," he said smugly.

"He's right, Axel."

Hugo chuckled. "Listen to your wife like a good little boy."

Axel fired a shot into his leg, and he screamed in pain. His men tried to run to him, but Axel raised his gun.

One way or another, this bullshit ended now. "Take out your phone," I demanded.

"No," he gritted as his wound poured with blood.

"He may have put Soren onto us. He followed me into the mall earlier," I told Axel, trying to get him to calm down and think rationally. Killing Hugo was not beneficial when too many pieces were missing from the puzzle.

"My wife just saved your life, but let me be clear. You're going to die." Axel struck Hugo across the face with the gun. "Now get out."

"This isn't over," Hugo seethed as blood dripped down his chin.

His men helped him out of the chair and escorted him from the warehouse.

I turned to face Axel and took the gun from him. "Big move, baby."

"Only move we needed to take. Put them all on notice. No more hiding." He pressed a kiss on my cheek and ran his hand down my back.

"He and Connor might become best friends over the idea of killing us."

Axel squeezed my ass. "Let them. Turin put a tracker on his car and now we have the upper hand."

Our men cleaned up the area as we left the warehouse headed to our car. We headed home to relax and wait for Hugo to make his next move.

* * *

When we got home, Axel disappeared into his office and I went to shower the day off without him trying to join me and distract me with sex. I was still sore from our last session and I just wanted to cuddle tonight in bed. The doctor had finally scheduled my appointment for birth control and I couldn't wait to get on the pill again. I didn't want to get pregnant before we'd handled Dario.

I dried off, wrapped my hair in a tight bun, and pulled on shorts and a t-shirt for the rest of the evening.

My phone rang, and I grabbed it from my purse. Heavy breathing came over the line.

"He can't save you."

"Dario?"

"Too many got in the way of what we had."

"We never had anything."

"Shut the fuck up!"

I ended the call, but it rang again immediately.

I took a moment to gather my thoughts before answering. "Hello."

"Where's my money?"

"Do you miss your little girlfriend, Dario?"

"My money, Gigi."

"I'll give you credit, Dario. You had people fooled, but I saw the real devil living inside you."

"Where's your little boy, Gigi?"

I dropped the phone and ran from the bedroom to his room. His crib was empty.

"Gaspare!" I screamed his name and sprinted down the stairs to the playroom. I burst through the door to see him in the swing with the nanny, who was reading him a book.

"Is everything all right, Mrs. Bresciani?" she questioned.

Gaspare burst into tears, and I felt bad for disturbing his peace. I couldn't shake the feeling that Dario had done something.

I took him from the nanny and kissed his warm

cheeks, wiping away his tears. I rocked him to calm him. "I'm sorry, baby bear. Mommy's sorry."

Axel ran into the room with his gun raised. "What's wrong? Did something happen?" He holstered his gun and charged toward, taking Gaspare from my arms to check him over.

"He's fine. I had a nightmare," I lied, my nerves raw.

"Can you give us a minute?" he asked the nanny.

She nodded and left the room. I sat on the couch to catch my breath. My hands shook and my heart raced. I closed my eyes and took some deep breaths.

"Dario called, and he asked about Gaspare. I got scared that he'd done something, so I ran to find him," I explained.

Axel pulled me off the couch to stand and rubbed my back. "Dario's time is up. I promise. He's playing mind games."

"It's working."

Axel looked at our son. "Gaspare is ready for a nap, and I'm ready to spend time with my wife."

Chapter 16

Gigi

Axel stuck to his promise and let me handle how I would approach the final moments with Ginerva. The day dawned like any other. The sun was shining, and a light breeze stirred the air, but I couldn't enjoy it. My heart was breaking and my hands were sweaty with the knowledge of what was to come.

Will I regret taking a life that meant so much to me growing up?

The warehouse was on lockdown, with only a handful of trusted soldiers on duty. I knew they were waiting for me to make a move, but I needed answers before I made the call.

Looking at Ginerva now, I could see that she lacked any remorse. I'd spent months trying to help her family find her, only to discover she was living with Dario.

Ginerva raised her chin, her eyes flashing fire. "He loves me."

Dario had her believing everything that came out of his mouth. She'd allowed his lies to cripple our relationship. Ginerva had let him destroy my family, and for that, she would have to pay.

"We had everyone looking for you," I told her.

She pressed her lips together.

"We did everything together, and you were sleeping with Dario Ramini behind my back." I laughed without humor.

"He wanted me first!" she yelled.

I ignored her outburst. "How do you expect me to forgive you?"

"You never loved Dario. Your engagement was a business arrangement."

"It was, but you know what our relationship was, and I hate to think about the lies you've told me."

She cackled and tugged at the ropes binding her wrists.

"All the times you were out with him but told me it was your fiancé." I tilted my head and glared at her.

"Dario said you never had sex with him. A man like him has needs."

I moved closer and cupped her chin, lifting her face to mine. "Janice told me about a bruise on your face."

Ginerva yanked her head away. "He never hit me."

"Do you think he's going to come and rescue you?"

"We could have been married."

I laughed. "I bet you would've slept with him even after we married."

"Dario is going to kill you and become the Boss. Then, he'll marry me."

"Marry you? How naïve are you, Ginerva?"

"He brought you along for the sex. Nothing about you will fulfil him."

"Dario told me that Axel's abusive."

"Please tell me when Axel was abusive."

"Let me go!"

"No."

"I covered so much for you with your parents. You owe me," she seethed.

"My parents have nothing to do with us."

"Please. You've always been dramatic and spoiled. Your parents gave you everything you wanted."

Her head snapped back from the force of my hand as I slapped her face. "The man killed my fucking family! He had my father killed and almost kill my husband and me. He's threatened my son!"

"Once Dario gets the Irish and Mendoza on his side, you'll beg for my help," she spat.

"You think I'm just gonna let you run off and be happy? You're delusional, Ginerva."

"Where is he?" Axel demanded.

"I don't know."

"He left you to die alone." Axel reminded her.

I threw my hands in the air. "He's gonna leave you to take your last breath alone, Ginerva."

"Gigi, don't, please. What about my family?" Ginerva begged.

"What about them? You weren't thinking about them before." I gestured to Onyx to remove her from the chair and put her on the table.

"Hold up! Wait!" She tried to fight, and he smacked her across the face.

I shook my head. "You decided to work with Dario."

"Okay! Okay!"

"Too late."

"Please, give me one more chance!" Ginerva begged.

I stood back and watched Axel pick up a saw and move toward her, while Onyx tied her to the table.

I turned my head to avoid her sorrowful look.

"Stop! No! My leg!" she screamed and suddenly went silent.

I turned to see she'd passed out.

"Wake her up," I commanded.

"Can you handle this, Gigi?" Axel asked, studying my face.

Nothing would distract me from what needed to be done. "Cut her arms next."

Ginerva woke groggily.

I marched to the table. "Where is Dario?"

"I... I... do-"

"I treated you like a sister."

She shivered. "I hate you."

I caressed her hair. "Neither hate nor love live in my heart anymore for you."

"He booked a flight to get out of town," she mumbled weakly.

I kissed her forehead.

"Kill her."

* * *

Onyx, Axel, and I jumped in the car to make in it time before Dario flew out of town. Traffic was busy during this time of day. Axel was on the phone to his soldiers, telling them to get to the private airport we knew Dario would use. I held onto the door handle as Onyx cut off cars and hopped on the freeway.

Axel handed me a gun. "In case you need to protect yourself."

I leaned forward and kissed him. "Be careful."

He winked at me.

Thirty minutes went by before Onyx sped through the security gate. My heart was resolute at the thought of Dario taking his last breath. All the lies, the manipulation of my father, the arranged marriage deal that was sealed years ago would end today. He wouldn't haunt my dreams anymore.

Axel pointed up ahead. Here was my chance to show Dario, my father, and Axel that I'd completed my mission of vengeance. I was married and a new mother, but I could handle the business of the Carrington Cartel. Dario hadn't defeated me.

The car whizzed down the road, and Onyx swerved around to the back of the airstrip.

"Send men on the other side, and we'll take the front," Axel stated.

"I want Dario taken alive," I reminded them.

"You ready?" Axel cocked his gun.

We ducked as gunfire exploded and Dario's guys shot at our cars.

"Stay down!" Axel yelled.

"Hold on!" Onyx reversed while Axel fired toward Dario.

I got on the other side and did the same.

Onyx turned the car to block the plane from leaving the runway. Axel and Onyx jumped out while I covered the rear. Axel walked alongside the plane, and I shot another solider when she tried to run up on Axel from behind.

"Watch out, Axel!" I picked up the dead soldier's AK 47 and shot the windows and tires of the plane.

Axel grabbed me and looked into my eyes. "You

good?" he asked, out of breath.

"Great. Let's go." I crushed my lips to his.

Onyx shot the guard at the plane door. Axel yanked the door open and Onyx went first and shot the flight attendant.

Onyx checked his watch. "We've got a few minutes before we need to get out of here and employees come looking."

Axel pointed the gun at Dario and he threw his hands up in the air.

"Dario, why did you use Ginerva?"

"She was easy." He smirked, showing no remorse.

The Casella family and Mendoza probably had him set to fly to Chicago or Italy if we hadn't stopped him today. All the deaths that followed him would see him in hell when we were finished with him. But first, I needed answers about Detective Soren and the Casella Cartel's role in all this.

Axel motioned for Dario to stand and dragged him off the plane. More bullets flew past us. Mendoza had Dario more protected than his nephew. I directed my soldiers to split up while we got him loaded in the car.

Dario's man was injured, and Onyx shot him in the head as he fell to the ground. I climbed in the back of the car and Ralfie headed away from the airstrip. Axel pulled out his phone and started texting. I stared out of the window as we drove out of the area before the cops arrived.

* * *

Axel nudged his phone in my face with a text from Antonio.

Antonio: *Clear.*

Axel: *Pulling up now.*

I nodded, relieved to finally finish what we'd started. We came around back, and I waited in the car while the men pulled Dario out in handcuffs with a bag over his head. Axel talked with Carlo at the door and waved for me to get out of the car.

Ralfie held it open and Axel's hand grasped my neck. "You up for what's going to happen?"

"Very much ready to end him."

Carlo and Axel escorted me inside and walked to the bar. Carlo motioned for his bartender to pour a drink. Carlo and Axel ordered food, but I was on pins and needles.

An hour passed with Dario loc up in Ryde nightclub's basement. Antonio said we needed discretion, since Detective Soren had already sniffed around our warehouses. I couldn't wait to hear what Dario had to say to explain his choices.

The door to Antonio's office closed and Axel kissed my head.

"Any word yet?"

"No. Mendoza hasn't called, or Soren."

"Then we can handle him now?"

Axel calmly lifted me from the seat and pulled me to the couch with me on his lap. "Soon as the club shuts down."

"That's a few hours from now."

"I know, but the staff is still lingering."

I was impatient and ready to get things over with. I leaned my head on his shoulder. "Soren will go nuts."

"He's the least of my worries."

The door flew open to Onyx and Ralfie with glares on their faces.

"What's wrong?" I asked.

Onyx said, "He's not talking."

Axel snaked his arm around my waist.

Onyx held up his phone. "Dario's people made some threats."

I saw a text from someone unknown discussing Dario missing. "Casella's men and Mendoza have no idea we have him."

"Unless Soren made him aware."

"You want to wait or kill him now?" I asked Axel.

"Let's do it." Axel grabbed my hand, and we took the elevator to the underground basement.

The door opened and Axel stepped into the room.

Ralfie looked down at his phone and scowled. "He's outside."

"Who?" Axel grew agitated.

"Detective Soren," he answered.

"We need to go see what he wants before Antonio shuts the place down with blood and we have more police in our business."

As we took the elevator to the main floor, I had a gut feeling Soren was trying to buy time for Dario. If he only knew it would lead to his own demise. As we got to the front, we saw it was surrounded by police and in the middle of them was Soren.

"I know he's here," Soren declared.

"Who?" I asked.

He crossed his arms over his chest. "A call came in of shots at a private airport and it seems the passenger was one Dario Ramini."

I shrugged. "What does that have to do with us?"

Detective Soren got in my face, but Axel pulled me behind him.

"If you have questions, take them up with our lawyer," Axel snapped at the detective.

"We have a search warrant."

"Go ahead. You won't find anything," Carlo announced.

The elevator was behind a wall that looked like a janitorial closet. No one expected there would be a secret trap in a club.

"You two need to come down to the station to answer some questions."

I narrowed my eyes. "What are we being charged with?"

"Conspiracy to commit murder, RICO charges, and drug trafficking."

I burst into laughter. "Where's the evidence, Detective? Or are you going by a 'he said' type of thing?" I mocked him.

"Take them in and search the place." Soren ignored my question and motioned for us to be handcuffed.

"If we're not being charged, we can drive ourselves," I countered.

Soren went to grab me, but Axel charged and punched him in the face.

"Fuck! Grab him," Detective Soren shouted. Two officers pulled Axel off him.

"Get the fuck away from my wife!" Axel grunted.

I stared into his eyes to get him to calm down. I knew Soren would use the punch as ammunition to get us locked up.

"Baby, I'm fine. I promise."

The look in his eyes was that of a man sick of people trying to keep us apart and destroy our lives.

Carlo and Ralfie talked him down and helped us out of the club with no further incidents. I took my phone and called our lawyer to meet us at the station. Two police officers escorted us into the station before Detective Soren and Raymond came to the door and watched me.

I lingered in the room alone while they held Axel in another area. We hadn't been charged or finger printed. No water or food was offered, and I knew they wanted to keep us in suspense. Finally, they seemed to have enough of me pacing, and Soren and Raymond came in and shut the door while a guard stood in the corner.

"You think as a mafia Boss you can get away with killing people at an airstrip and no one notices?" Soren demanded.

"I'm not talking to anyone until I speak with my lawyer and my husband."

"He's busy."

"Where is Axel?"

"Tied up," Soren muttered with a satisfied look.

"If anything happens to him—"

"Are you threatening an officer?"

"Sounds like she's putting a hit out on you," Raymond responded.

I scoffed at the feeble attempt to trap me.

"Where is Dario Ramini?" Soren questioned.

"Hopefully in hell."

"You think this is fun and games?"

"What I know and think are two different things, Detective."

"Women like you make me sick."

"So you have mommy issues. A woman broke your

heart. Your parents didn't love you enough." I ran off scenarios and his nostrils flared.

"Dario was an informant for the police," Raymond explained.

"Why are you telling me?"

"If something happens to him and we find out it was you..." Raymond let his words trail off ominously.

"Nothing for me to say. I haven't talked to Dario in months."

"He goes missing right when a flight is supposed to take off?"

"Again, I have no clue."

"She's lying." Soren slammed his hand on the table.

"How would you know unless you've been following me, Detective? Stalking and harassment is against the law."

Soren stood, threw the chair into the corner, and charged at me. Raymond blocked him before he could touch me.

"Bitch. You're not innocent," Soren growled.

I smiled. "Dario had the same expression the last time I talked to him."

The room went still as the door flew open to my lawyer and Axel. Raymond pushed Soren back and Axel marched toward me. He smoothed his hands up and down my arms, checking my face for any bruises.

Soren said, "Dead bodies were found at the airstrip."

"Tragic," I replied.

"No witnesses. We received a call from an employee. We discover it's connected to a mob cartel, and you want me to let her go?" Soren muttered to my lawyer.

"There is no evidence linking my client to any of this," John challenged.

I stood. "Can we go? I need to get home to my son."

"This isn't over," Raymond hissed.

Axel kept his eyes on Soren and Raymond as I walked out of the interrogation room and down the corridor.

"Keep walking," John said, leading us outside.

"Soren is like a bomb ready to explode at any moment," Axel muttered.

"How did you get us out?" I asked.

"I have evidence that you guys were traveling to take a flight and came upon a situation." John grinned.

Axel shook hands with him before helping me into the waiting town car. I clung to Axel's side as he slid in beside me.

"Are you all right? Are you hurt?" he asked.

"No, I'm fine. We need to get to Dario and finish him."

"I agree. Let's go." He nodded at Ralfie to drive.

Everybody piled in their cars and drove back to Antonio's club to finish putting out the trash.

The forty-minute drive gave me time to decide how I'd like to spread out Dario's torture and pain, but another part of me wanted to put a bullet straight through his brain. After all, he didn't show my family mercy.

* * *

Seconds after we made it back to the club, John gave us the rundown on keeping things clean so Soren wouldn't return to harass us. Axel shook his hand, and I waved goodbye before we walked back into the club.

The bartender chucked his chin at us, and we stepped into the elevator to head down to the basement. My stomach was queasy at the thought of killing the person who had torched my life.

Ralfie stepped aside when the elevator doors opened and let us approach first. I heard screams. The door was open, and Dario and Mendoza's men were on the floor with their hands tied behind their back. I looked into Dario's empty eyes and wondered if he had any regrets. The little girl in me who grew up with Dario felt bad, but she needed to stay locked away because at one time I did care for him as a family friend.

Turin whistled, and the guards stepped away from Dario. I moved closer to see the bruises they'd put on his face. I'd demanded they leave his death to me.

Chapter 17

Axel

She held her head high, her entire body stoic and commanding. I knew I couldn't take this moment away from her. Gigi needed this closure in order for us to move on and be a family, to not have enemies who wanted us dead. As her husband, I watched and gave her what she needed—control of Dario's last breath.

I stood back and watched as she sauntered toward him. She clipped his chin and peeped into his eyes, and I wanted to pull them out of his head. After everything he'd done, he deserved it. But I couldn't get too overwhelmed. Today was Gigi's closure.

"You think she's going to be okay?" Onyx asked.

"After we finish everything, I do."

"Soren and Mendoza?"

My top lip twitched. "Both need to die for threatening my family."

Onyx said, "He never talked."

"We're trained not to talk."

"Soren didn't find anything when they searched," Turin said.

"Did Antonio come down?" I asked.

Turin shook his head. "No. Carlo let him know we handled Soren. Is retirement still a go?"

"After this, I think she will. But it's her choice. Gigi was controlled by her parents. I don't want to be that way with her." I was pretty close to losing her at the airstrip, then with Soren arresting us.

The conversation in the room brought me back to the issue at hand.

"Tell me the truth, Dario," Gigi demanded.

"Everything you have was meant for me. You are too stupid, too naïve, and too precious as Laurent's daughter to see the bigger picture," Dario taunted, looking from Gigi to me.

I clenched my jaw, ready to punch his teeth out.

"You killed my mother and father. For money and power. It's all about power." Gigi balled up her fists.

Dario threw his head back dramatically. "God, stop being naïve. You're doing the same thing."

"I didn't kill to get there," Gigi hissed.

He licked his lips and blew a kiss. "Ginerva understands the legacy of the cartel. She gave me what I wanted."

"You used her to get to me. For power you didn't have, so you could kill my father."

"Laurent wouldn't have let me lead the way I wanted to. He wouldn't let go. He wanted control even when he retired. I had other plans."

"Well, lucky you. I have other plans, too."

She picked up the knife and plunged it into his stomach.

Dario cried out and tried to move away. Gigi pulled the knife out and plunged it into his shoulder. She dropped the knife on the ground, reached for the gun, and moved back a few steps.

Gigi shot him twice in the knee caps.

"Bitch!" he screamed.

"Power will always be up for grabs when it comes to the cartel. You only achieve loyalty and power from the people who believe in your shared goals. I led my cartel with loyalty, and they devoted their lives to me. Tell Rosa she didn't win."

Gigi pushed the button, and a small steel door opened to a fire Antonio used to destroy any evidence when doing business around the building.

Dario tried to wiggle away, but our men ensured he was strapped tight when they laid him on top of the table and watched him burn alive. One after the other, we took care of each goon, listening to their screams as they died.

When Gigi was ready to leave, Turin stayed to clean up and ensure there were no traces of us ever being there.

* * *

I slipped the key in the door soon as we got out of the car and made it home. Gigi rolled her neck, and I drew her in close, kissing her head.

"Let me check on Gaspare." Gigi yawned.

I smoothed my hands along her back. "I'll run a bath for you."

Gigi nodded and walked off. I set the alarm and headed to the bar. Grabbing the bottle of cognac, I poured a glass and went upstairs. I unbuttoned my shirt on the way to the bathroom and turned the light on. Placing the glass on the counter, I kicked off my shoes and turned the faucet on to fill the jacuzzi tub. I poured Gigi's favorite lavender and vanilla bubble bath soap into the water.

Gigi appeared as I lit the last candle and I helped her undress and climb into the water to relax and let the day go.

"Detective Soren," she murmured.

I kissed her forehead. "Shush... relax for me."

She gazed into my eyes. "Are you heading back out tonight?"

"No, I'm here for the night. Turin can handle the cleanup."

"I feel a weight lifted off our shoulders."

"He can't hurt you anymore."

"He had no remorse."

"People like him never do."

"Get in the water with me."

I bent over the tub and nibbled on her bottom lip. "If I get in the water, more than relaxing is going to happen."

"A little relaxation in the form of you inside me could help."

"I love you," I growled.

"Hearing you say and prove your love is all I ever need in life."

Her words caused warmth to spread in my chest and my dick to twitch. Hurriedly, I removed my clothes and stepped into the large jacuzzi tub, helping Gigi climb on top of my lap. Slowly, she reached in between us and placed my rod at her entrance. We felt the contact immediately, and needed a moment before we could move. With her full breasts and doe-eyes filled with lust, I couldn't help but want to dominate her tonight.

She leaned forward and kissed me on the lips once,

twice, until I caught her tongue. I gripped her ass cheeks and rocked her slowly back and forth.

"Feel our connection," Gigi whispered, nuzzling her face along my shoulder and neck.

"Ah, fuck."

"Oh, god, baby," she moaned.

Our bodies formed a rhythm and slapped against the water as our sighs filled the room. I gathered her hair in my hand and tugged her head back, sucking, licking, and nibbling my way down to her breasts.

Gigi cried out, "Fuck! I feel you, baby."

Ready to take her to bed, I removed the plug from the tub. Lifting her in my arms, I carefully stepped out of the tub and walked to the bedroom. We were still soaking wet as I planted her on the bed. I sucked her nipple as I grasped her leg and slid back into her warm, tight hole.

"Like it was the first time," I muttered, picking up my thrusts.

I scanned down our bodies, watching her sex contort as I pushed her legs back to her chest and pumped in and out.

"Yes, Axel! Keep going."

"I swear to love you forever, baby. Fuck! I'm gonna come."

"Come inside me, please," she begged as her soft hands rubbed up and down my back.

I squeezed my eyes shut and released inside her pussy as we kissed. Soon after, she straddled me and put her feet flat on the bed, moving herself up and down.

I smacked her ass and pushed her breasts together and she came with a long moan. She fell forward and pressed her lips to mine as her movements slowed.

We made love for the rest of the night.

* * *

The next morning, I had Turin meet me at the office to go over the plan for dealing with Detectives Soren and Raymond. All the information had finally come in, and we knew he was Dario's cousin. It was why he'd been stalking my family. The contact Laurent used in the past was sent to me to do his job. The chief of police tried to avoid us, but Antonio let him know what needed to be done or he would be handled directly. We'd have more eyes on us when they went missing, but we'd paid enough people to look the other way.

"You've never had a problem with handling a coverup," Antonio told the chief as we sat in my office.

The chief fidgeted in his seat. "That was before more bodies went missing at the hands of the Carrington Cartel."

"Either you get rid of him or we will."

The chief grumbled, "It's not easy removing two detectives."

"Perhaps you could send them on an assignment that goes tragically wrong."

"Your family made a bigger problem when you landed here. I'll do what I can, but it's going to take time." He blew out a breath.

"We don't have time." I slammed my hand on the desk.

"Soren won't be a problem for much longer." The chief held up his hands.

I pointed at his face. "He's trying to make a name for himself. Being related to Dario should help speed up the process of his cases being looked at for bias."

The chief ran a hand down the back of his neck. "Give me a few days."

"You have twenty-fours."

"Either your family or Detective Soren," I stated.

"He's too high-profile right now," the chief argued.

"All the more reason to take him out." I gritted my teeth.

The chief nodded, picked up the file, and turned to leave the office. I kept my eyes on him when Gigi passed him in the hallway.

"You think he's going to do his job?" Turin inquired.

"No reason not to believe him."

Gigi pushed the door open with a look of gloom on her face. "What was the Chief doing here?"

"Taking care of a rat," I replied.

"Oh, well, I wanted to tell you I need to run out for a moment before my meeting."

"Is everything good?"

Turin stepped out of the room and gave us some privacy.

Gigi looked everywhere but at me.

"If something is bothering you, I need to know."

"Stop worrying. Can you pick up Gaspare from the park? The nanny has to take her mom to the doctor," Gigi informed me.

I nodded and as soon as she left, I met Turin outside in the car and headed to the park. My phone vibrated, and I pulled it from my pocket.

Mendoza: *Two down. You'll still end up losing.*

Me: *You're on borrowed time.*

Mendoza: *Fuck you.*

Me: *I only do that with my wife.*

Mendoza: *Casella may have left, but I'll get what's mine.*

Me: *Try me.*

"That look on your face says you're ready to kill," Turin remarked.

"Mendoza pisses me off." I sent a message to our tech to pinpoint his location.

"He's back in Chicago," Turin added.

"How do you know?"

Turin shrugged. "I've been keeping an eye on him."

"So he ran off after finding out Dario was dead?"

"Probably, plus Casella's people decided to make other arrangements."

"We need to make plans to visit the Windy City."

"Already went to the windy city with your wife."

"And we all know how that turned out."

"She killed the nephew, and you kill the uncle. Can't take either of you anywhere."

I chuckled. "They say a couple acts alike after a while."

We reached the park, and I opened the door to meet our nanny halfway with Gaspare. Turin popped the trunk and grabbed his baby bags.

"He ate an hour ago," the nanny said.

I rocked him in my arms and he smiled at me. "Great, I'll let his mom know and you can take the rest of the day off."

"Thank you, sir."

I nodded and watched her get in her car.

"Where now?" Turin asked.

"Home. I need to make sure the chief does what he promised."

"He's not stupid."

"All of them are at some point."

Mendoza thought I was letting our dealings go without payback because we hadn't immediately gone after him. I liked to keep people waiting until they got comfortable before I helped them to leave the earth.

Once I got Gaspare settled, I called to check on Gigi, but the phone went straight to voicemail. I hung up and dialed again from my office phone.

"*I can't come to the phone right now. Please leave a message.*"

I pulled up the location from the app we shared on my phone and saw she was at Janice's home. I'd give her a few minutes before I jumped in my car to bring her back.

My phone rang, and I recognized the chief's number. "Is it done?"

"In all my years of being a police officer, I can count on one hand how many times I've had to eliminate a fellow officer."

"Don't feel bad. It was him or you."

"That's not funny," the chief argued.

"Not meant to be."

"He's going to turn up in a motel dead from an overdose."

"Send me the location and who called it in?"

"A few junkies." The chief rambled off the location.

I typed it in my cell, grabbed my jacket, and left the house manager to keep an eye on Gaspare. Turin wouldn't be needed while I made a run to check on Detective Soren's final resting place. I sped down the freeway for an hour toward Brooklyn and was greeted by police cars and ambulances out front. I parked and jumped out, closing in on the reporters and nosy neighbors speculating about what had happened.

"What happened here?"

An older woman in a postal uniform eyed me before she answered. "Some police officer was found dead."

"Alone?"

"Probably a drug bust gone wrong. This neighborhood has so much going on. I'm not surprised."

"Tough times."

I turned to go back to my car, tipping my head to the chief standing in the corner with fellow officers. The body was rolled out of the motel in a body bag.

My phone rang, and I snapped it to my ear. "You home?"

"Yes, and you're not here," Gigi said softly.

"Had to handle something."

"Should I be worried?"

"No, all our problems are being solved."

"Well not all."

I climbed into the car and slid the key into the ignition.

I startled as someone banged on the window. I looked to see Raymond trying to open my door.

"What the fuck?"

"Axel? What's that noise?"

"I'll call you back."

"No! Stay on the phone with me."

I pushed the door open and tossed the phone aside. "The fuck is your problem?" I shouted, shoving him in the chest.

"I know you killed him," Raymond snarled.

"Raymond, calm down." The chief marched over to us.

"Listen to your boss."

"Fuck you. He told me you'd be responsible if anything happened to him," Raymond hissed.

"Throwing around accusations like that could get you in trouble, Detective."

"Chief, arrest him!"

"Raymond, you need to calm down and go sit in the car," the chief demanded.

"He needs to be off the streets. Dario Ramini goes missing, and Soren is dead."

"Maybe they're together." I grinned.

Raymond didn't like my snarky reply and lunged at me. I stepped aside, and he collided with my car.

"You've been drinking, Detective," the chief saidand motioned for his men to take Raymond away.

I waited for him to leave and glared at the chief. "I told you to take care of them both."

"He was held up," the chief mumbled.

I poked him in the chest. "Fix it, or you'll be next on the news."

"Give me a few days. It'll look weird if both detectives end up dead," the chief grumbled.

I saw his point, but the last thing on my mind was how the optics looked. His job was to take care of our problems. The cartel made him a lot of money and put him in places he wouldn't be otherwise, socializing with political leaders.

I nodded. "One more day."

Chapter 18

Gigi

I lay on the cold bed and waited for the doctor to return with my blood test results. I hadn't felt good for a while, and I knew why, but I was in denial. Axel and I hadn't been careful at all and ignored my six weeks. The idea of being pregnant again was nerve-racking. No matter what, I would love my child, but two babies close together was stressful. Plus, starting a new business was on my list of things I wanted to do. The thought of having two kids to run behind, all while tending to a husband and my personal needs, made me anxious.

"Well, you were right to come in for a checkup," the doctor said as she entered the room.

I blew out a shaky breath. "Tell me."

"Congratulations. You're pregnant."

I removed my feet from the stirrups and groaned. I was more scared of being pregnant than murdering someone. "Oh god. I knew it."

"Young couples tend to ignore the six weeks."

"My husband for sure didn't care."

She laughed, and I joined in. I knew Axel would love this news.

"You're a great mom, so this one will be blessed."

"Thank you, Doctor. I'm just stressed because Gaspare is so young."

"Try not to worry, and maybe take a vacation."

"I'll think about that."

"Make another appointment in a few weeks."

She left, and I climbed off the table and dressed. I grabbed my phone, debating whether to tell Axel now or wait and surprise him.

My phone vibrated in my hand and I saw Axel's name. Speak of the devil.

"Hello."

"You on your way home?"

"About to leave the doctor's office now."

"Gaspare misses you."

I smile. "Just Gaspare?"

"Come find out." Axel suggested.

I nodded at Ralfie and climbed in the back. He shut the door, climbed behind the wheel, and started the car.

"What did the doc say?" Axel asked.

"I'm fine."

"Good."

I released my breath. "I'm pregnant."

The phone grew quiet. "Pregnant?"

"Yes. How do you feel?"

"I expect you're not too happy, but I'm overjoyed." Axel said quietly.

I groaned and threw my head back. "You couldn't wait and now we'll have two kids under the age of two."

He chuckled. "We can handle it."

"Not funny, Axel."

"Life is funny like that, baby."

"Well, you should have kept your hands to yourself."

He chuckled again. "Get home safe."

"You, too."

"I need to get Gaspare home before he cries my ears off."

"Okay. I'll probably call the girls over to hangout."

"That's fine. See you later."

"See you later. Be safe."

"You too, *mi amore*."

Ralfie whisked us back to the house while I thought about what our next child would look like. I'd fallen instantly in love with Gaspare, and I wondered if my love would grow to include another child. Would I be able to balance everything with two?

Ralfie parked the car and opened my door. I thanked him entered the house to find Janice and Sabrina already there.

"What in the world are you two doing here?" I hugged both ladies.

"Axel told us you had a doctor's appointment today and wanted us to be here when you made it home," Janice said.

"I just got off the phone with him and said I would call you two."

"He figured, so we decided to surprise you instead." Sabrina grinned.

"I'm pregnant."

Janice smirked and sipped on her glass of mimosa. "You won't be drinking with us then."

"He's to blame." I pouted and followed them into the kitchen where Ebony had food displayed across the island.

"Blame him all you want, but your legs stayed open twenty-four-seven for that man," Janice joked.

I flipped her off. "Coming from you, that means a lot,"

I laughed at her sly expression. Carlo would have a fleet of kids if Janice allowed it, but she had plans to enjoy her life once all the kids moved out.

"Sabrina, you're laughing a little too hard for my liking, ma'am." Janice poked her lip out and Sabrina cackled. She and Antonio had five kids.

Sabrina hunched her shoulders and picked up a plate of waffles and fruit. "You'll have two babies while you're still young. I know it can be scary, but we're here to help."

"Thanks. Remember I told you I wanted to start my charity work?"

"Yes. Did you get the paperwork started?" Janice queried.

"My lawyer is sending everything over for me after he files."

Sabrina nodded. "Axel's fine with you working?"

"Charity work is better than me sticking with cartel life."

"True, and we work normal jobs. Never missed being in the men's business once we left," Janice said.

"Dario and Ginerva are dealt with now," I confirmed.

Sabrina shook her head. "Hard to believe she'd been holding on to so much hate for you."

No more pretending she cared about our friendship. "Yeah. I'm glad I'll never see the look of disgust in her eyes again."

The memory of Ginerva's hate for me would probably haunt me for a while, but the realization that I needed to protect myself and family came first. I was right about leaving the cartel behind.

"Have you picked out a location?" Janice asked.

I cut into my pancakes and took a bite. "A place that's at least two stories, maybe three. And not too far from home, so the travel isn't rough with me being home on time for Gaspare."

"We can talk to our realtor and look at commercial property," Sabrina suggested.

"Wonderful. I appreciate the help."

"If you need donations, please hit me up. I'd love to run Carlo's pockets." Janice smirked.

"Carlo is going to put you on an allowance," I chuckled.

She lifted her glass and refilled it for a second round of mimosa. "Carlo will never put me on an allowance if he wants to sleep with both eyes closed."

"You threaten that man so much," I quipped.

Janice brushed us off. "He likes it. It's my love language."

Sabrina choked on her drink, and Janice and I burst into laughter. You never knew what would come out of her mouth.

Janice tapped on her phone while Sabrina and I talked about the realtor she could put me in touch with to look at spaces. A few moments later, the door opened and Axel and Turin walked in.

"Ladies," Axel greeted, bending to kiss my cheek.

"Axel, tell your friend, Carlo, he'd better answer my phone calls," Janice said, hopping off the stool with her phone to her ear as she waited for him to answer. Those two went back and forth all the time.

Axel took a bite of my food and caressed my cheek. "How's my baby doing?"

"I'm a few seconds pregnant," I dryly answered.

He smirked, and I rolled my eyes.

"Reminds me of when Antonio got me pregnant back-to-back." Sabrina sighed.

"He knew what he was doing." I gulped my orange juice.

"I'm taking Gigi to look at property if you can spare her for a few hours?" Sabrina put her plate in the sink and I followed. Our housekeeper would take care of the dishes once everyone was cleared out.

"Do you mind if I step out? I could wait and go tomorrow, but I need to keep my mind distracted."

"No, go ahead. Keep the guards with you. Still have to be careful."

He interlocked our hands and kissed me twice before he smacked me on the butt and let me go.

* * *

A week later, I stood around the table with our men and waited for them to quiet before we discussed the news.

"Casella is back in Italy."

"What about Mendoza?" one of my men asked.

All eyes focused on Axel and me.

"He's in Chicago, still trying to get support to take us out," Axel replied.

"And you are not willing to deal with him?"

I cleared my throat. "Pointless, but that's not the only thing we need to talk about."

"Anything to do with cops looking for Dario Ramini?" another of my men questioned.

"Dario is no longer a concern, but I'm pregnant."

The room went silent.

"What does this mean?" The man's eyes narrowed.

We made them a lot of money and gave them a generous percentage when doing business. I figured they were nervous that if I left the business, the new Boss would cut them out of deals. I lifted my eyes to Axel. I didn't need his permission. But I liked to get his thoughts and opinions. Like me, he hated to be questioned about how we ran our business.

"I'm stepping down."

"Who will run the Carrington Cartel?"

"Me," Axel answered.

"As the enforcer of the cartel, shouldn't you stick to that role?" our talkative friend asked.

"Axel is more than capable of handling the role of leader—"

Axel raised his hand to cut me off. "The business will remain true to what Laurent put in place. But let me be very clear; loyalty is to this family."

Axel made eye contact with everyone in the room. Tension was high, but no one replied and all nodded in agreement.

We left together, and I expressed my gratitude for his support in the limo. We pulled up at the building I wanted to get his opinion on before I made the big purchase.

We got out of the limo and Axel scanned the area. "The outside looks good, and it's not a high traffic area."

"I asked the realtor to make sure the place wasn't in a bad area for my first building."

I'd decided to open a child center. I was blessed growing up with a staff of people surrounding me, and

Gaspare would have the same. The idea was to spread care and love to other families with a top-of-the-line facility where money wouldn't be a problem. The place would have every item a kid would love when not at home. The staff and parents would be comfortable and know we took pride in wanting the kids to be safe and loved like they were our own.

Axel walked around the front and noticed the open space and large windows.

I stood in the back and watched him look around the room. "Too much?"

"No. If you like it, get it."

I clapped my hands together. "I have so many plans. I'll have an office, but I know I can't be here every day."

"Correct. You're still the wife of the Don."

"I know, baby."

We kissed and made our way home to eat dinner and hang out with Gaspare.

Once we made it to bed, I slipped off my nightgown, trailed my lips across his jaw and down his neck. It had been a long day, touring the building and meeting with our men.

"I love you," I murmured.

"I love you, too."

Axel moved the phone toward me. "Last thing to handle before we're finished."

"Okay." I nodded in understanding.

I smiled and handed the phone back to him, staring at the pictures of Connor and Mendoza.

Chapter 19

Axel

Turin slipped the crates open. He picked up a Glock and looked it over before replacing it and motioning for the guys to seal it up.

The minute I announced I was taking over the cartel, there was nothing stopping me from making my rounds to every person we had business with. I promised Gigi I would be home soon, so this was the final stop of the day before heading home for the afternoon party.

Gigi and I never had a baby shower for Gaspare, so Janice and Sabrina had decided to throw a little gathering. At first, I wasn't onboard as we'd have a house full of people, but Gigi complained about tradition and how we should be able to do normal stuff like other couples with newborns. Rather than get in a shouting match, I gave in and left the planning to her and the girls.

"All solid," Turin announced.

"The minimum is ten crates." I glanced at Chauncey, a local gang leader in the city.

"I want twenty," Chauncey said.

I looked at Turin, who nodded. He'd heard of

Chauncey and knew how he did things in the Bronx. Antonio had sent word that he was clean and never had problems with his team.

"Twenty," I agreed.

"Monthly," Chauncey expressed.

"Long as you can pay the fee." I slipped my hands in my pockets.

"Money is no problem."

I removed my hand and stuck it out for him. "Then we have a deal, Chauncey." I gripped his hand tight and made eye contact. "I expect no problems."

He nodded and snapped his fingers for his team to bring the bags of money.

"Anything else will go through Turin. This is our first and last meeting," I announced.

"We're clear," Chauncey replied.

Turin and I strolled out of the building and headed toward the car. The car ride wouldn't take long, and I replied to a few emails on the legit businesses we had in the Carrington fold. The twenty minutes went fast and when I saw the red, white, and blue balloons outside our house, I knew Gigi had gone overboard with decorations.

Inside, I watched my son as he played with his toys. He had no clue why all these people were in his face. It wasn't his birthday, but Gigi thought gifts, music, and an ice sculpture made the perfect pick for a post baby shower.

"Ice sculpture?" I asked in disbelief.

"I love it. Look at the cake. They made it look exactly like Gaspare."

"He has no idea and won't remember this party."

"We have a videographer and photographer."

I picked up my son and nuzzled him close. "How much did it cost?"

Gigi wiped Gaspare's chin. "Not too much."

"How much?"

Gigi rolled her eyes. "Thirty thousand."

I chuckled. "I know I didn't hear thirty thousand."

"Axel, memories will last forever."

"Whatever you say, dear."

Gigi didn't need the stress of an argument, so I dropped the subject, but I would let Janice and Sabrina know to come to me next time when they got the idea to throw a party.

"Are you hungry?" Gigi asked, changing the subject.

"No. How are you feeling?"

"Fine."

"Have you eaten?"

"Not yet. I've been running around getting the party together."

"Come with me." I grasped her hand and walked us out of the living room to the backyard, where tables were set with food. I picked up a plate, filled it with food, and handed it to her.

Janice and a few kids were playing in the pool.

"You home for the rest of the day?" Gigi asked.

"Yeah. I finished my business."

"How did it go?"

"Nothing for you to worry about." I looked pointedly at her plate. "Eat."

"I can see how you'll be once the new baby comes," Gigi grumbled and dug into her salad.

"I missed the first pregnancy. I'm not missing the second one." I grinned and rubbed her stomach.

"Come sit with me." Gigi took my hand, walked over to the cabana at the side of the pool.

Gaspare reached for his mom while she ate, but I tucked him in my arms and let him play with the toy bear. "Who are these people?"

"Friends and extended family on my mom's side."

"You didn't tell me you stayed in contact with that side of the family."

Gigi shrugged and lifted her fork toward me to eat.

"You eat."

"I want Gaspare and this new baby to have as much family as possible. Have you thought about contacting some of your family?"

Gaspare bounced in my arms. "Never paid it any mind. A few people sent condolences, but no one stayed in contact. I needed an escape, and I did that when I became a part of the cartel."

"Well, Gaspare will have something neither of us got when we lost our parents."

"What?" My brow hiked up.

"A family full life of love and happiness." She leaned over and kissed me.

"How much longer is this going to go on?"

"So grumpy."

"Happy. You and my son are having fun, but I have work to do."

"It can't wait?"

"Not this."

Gigi tried to take Gaspare, but I stood up. "He's coming with me to the office."

"What about his party? We still need to open the gifts."

"Enjoy the party, Gigi. Gaspare only cares about

putting his hand in his mouth." I bent and pressed a kiss on her forehead. She muttered, and I smiled at her pout.

I left the party and shut the office door behind me. Gaspare fiddled with my cell phone as I turned on my computer and checked my emails.

The phone rang, and I took it from Gaspare's mouth. He whimpered, so I rocked him back and forth. *Probably should have given him to Gigi,* I thought.

"Everything set?" Antonio asked.

"Set and cleared."

"Chauncey won't be a problem?"

"No. Turin is back to full health and can handle the meetings."

"I hear congrats are in order."

"Gigi and the girls love to gossip."

Antonio chuckled. "My wife loves Gigi like a little sister."

"They've been supportive, and I appreciate the kindness with those other tasks."

"Don't mention it. New York is my home, and I welcome the Carringtons."

"Thanks."

"The mayor would like a meeting."

"Mayor?"

"A businessman like yourself could do great things in his city, and he'd like to schedule something for the future."

I sat back and pondered his statement. "The mayor knows I'm not foolish or naïve like Mendoza?"

"We've had a conversation." Antonio replied.

"I guess we'll have a sit down."

"Money moves in New York, and the mayor won't interrupt."

"Glad to hear it."

"I just got a text from my wife. She's on her way home."

"So that means I can have my wife back." I chuckled.

"Indeed." The dial tone served as a goodbye.

I looked at Gaspare asleep in my arms and ran a hand over his head. "One day, this will all be yours."

I finished reading over paperwork and emails. When I finished, I took Gaspare to the living room to find Gigi watching TV. "Party over?"

"Yes," Gigi watched as I placed Gaspare in the play pen to nap.

I sat close to her on the couch, reaching my arm around her and she leaned into my chest. "You have fun?"

"Fun as can be expected for a last-minute shower."

"The next baby will have a real one."

"Do you want a girl or boy?"

"I don't care so long as you're both healthy."

"Same." She yawned.

"I'm meeting with the mayor."

She jerked back at my statement. "Mayor? Why?"

"Business."

"Is he trying to do something?"

"Antonio arranged it and said he comes in peace."

"The mayor wanting to meet could be good for us. Help establish my business and you running the legit businesses on paper."

"More at stake."

Gigi placed a finger under my chin for a kiss. "He's not stupid enough to mess with you. How about we go out tonight?"

"The nanny?"

"She's asleep, but we can let her know we're going out. I want to go to Ryde tonight and dance."

"You know I'm not a club person."

Gigi rose from the couch. "But you promised to cherish your wife and spoil her, correct?"

I frowned. "That had nothing to do with going out to the club."

She grinned, wrapping her arms around my waist and standing on her tiptoes for a kiss. Our tongues danced, but before we got carried away, Gaspare started crying.

Gigi pulled back and picked him up. "See? Even he knows how to get what he wants from us."

* * *

It wasn't too crowded at the club. Ralfie turned off the engine, and I opened the door to help Gigi out. I held her close as the bouncer motioned us inside, and our private bottle girl walked us over to the VIP section. Antonio didn't get out much anymore, but he'd set us up and Carlo tagged along with Janice. Turin came without a date for protection, but Gigi kept trying to hook him up with women. Antonio and Sabrina stayed home to enjoy a night as a couple. In a few years, that would be Gigi and me when our kids went off to college and left the two of us alone.

My phone buzzed on the table and I lifted it to see the time and date of the meeting with the mayor. I extended it to Turin, and he noted it on his phone, then went to drink his beer.

"Are you going to sit here all night or will you dance with me?" Gigi spoke in my ear.

She was wearing a black halter dress with cut outs on

the sides that showed off her full breasts and thighs. I wanted to burn it when she put it on, but she begged to keep it, telling me I could rip it off her when we got home.

"Baby, I don't dance."

"What if another man asks me to dance?"

"That won't happen."

She grinned. "How do you know?"

"Everyone knows who you belong to, *Mrs. Bresciani*."

Gigi bit her bottom lip. She slid her hand down my chest to my groin and squeezed.

I stopped before she could go further and lifted her hand to my lips, kissing each finger. "You know I love you, right?"

"*Mi amore*," she whispered.

She stood when Janice came over, snapping her fingers to the music. I watched the crowd as Ralfie escorted the girls down to the dance floor with the other guards. She was protected at all times, but I had my hand on my gun as a precaution.

She did some number with her hips twisting to the side and turned around to face me. I knew she wanted to rile me up and get a reaction. I winked and continued to listen to the song playing from the DJ booth.

"Janice asked me about Gigi's birthday and if you're doing something special," Carlo said.

"We haven't had time to sit and discuss it."

Carlo clapped me on the shoulder. "Women's birthdays are important."

"You're right. My head's been deep into the cartel."

"My advice?" Carlo looked at the screens of the club. "Go ahead."

Carlo tipped his beer and took a sip. "Happy wife, happy life."

We still had a few weeks before her birthday. I planned on making her feel special and aware of how much Gaspare and I needed her in our lives. I had time to get something planned.

Dance after dance, Gigi enjoyed herself until she was ready to go home. She straddled my lap in the back of the limo, her palms on both sides of my face and her tongue down my throat. I slipped my hand under her dress and caressed her smooth skin. Her moans filled the car and my dick was ready to slide inside her hot pussy.

I gripped the back of her neck and pulled her head back to stare into her warm eyes. "You're pregnant."

"I am," she purred.

"My wife is pregnant with my baby."

She grinned. "Make love to me."

I buried my nose in her neck and smelled her perfume that drove me wild. "Fucking ready to taste you."

Gigi moaned when I squeezed her breast.

Chapter 20

Gigi

My plans came along great. I wanted each room to be a different theme, with security cameras inside and out. Being on the go for my new business felt good. I envisioned my schedule; up early to take calls, plan events, and visit with Gaspare so he could make friends. This could mean so much to families, and there was media interest in my new business venture. I enjoyed giving back and proving that a woman that could be a mother, wife, and business owner.

I turned to leave, and Ralfie opened the door. I took my cell out of my purse saw to see that Axel had sent a few messages while it was on silent.

Axel: Meet me at the boat dock at one.

I flipped my wrist to see the time was twelve-fifteen.

Me: Baby, I just got your message. I might be a few minutes late.

Axel: Bring your sexy ass. Be safe getting here.

I nibbled on my bottom lip and leaned forward in the limo. "Ralfie, take me to the boat dock at Waverly."

"Yes, ma'am," Ralfie answered.

A few months ago, Axel had rented a yacht for a night trip under the moon, food prepared by a chef, and a live band. It was the most fun I'd had for a long time. I was blissfully in love with a man who wasn't afraid to show me his flaws and his love for me was all-consuming.

Ralfie made it in a short time and passed through the gate to park. I looked out at the boats and saw the yacht he'd rented last time called Sunshine. Not waiting for Ralfie to open the door, I stepped out and darted down the boardwalk. The crew stood with a glass of cider, and I smiled as I took it from the brass tray.

"Thank you."

He smiled.

I headed up the steps and looked around. The place was decorated in gold signs that read *Congrats on Your Business*. I grinned and went inside to see the chef placing trays of food on the table.

"Mrs. B, how are you?" Sandy wiped the counter clean.

"Hi, Chef Sandy. I'm good."

"Please call me Sandy." She laughed.

"Call me Gigi, and we have a deal."

"You got it, Gigi."

"Everything looks amazing, as usual." I picked up an olive and popped it in my mouth.

Sandy laid out more food, from salad to a seafood bowl and cupcakes. "Mr. B said you'll be eating shortly."

"I'm going to go find him."

I grabbed a piece of shrimp and a napkin and went to look for Axel. Rose petals were scattered on the ground floor and I smirked as I went toward the bedroom on the next level. I heard music coming from the bedroom as I wrapped my hand around the door handle. I pushed it open and gasped. Tears pooled in my eyes when I saw the large sign on the wall.

Congrats to the best wife.

I set the drink down on the dresser. "You did this for me?"

Axel stood from the bed, holding a rose, and his eyes heated as he approached me. Our eyes connected as I latched onto his shoulders, and he held the flower under my nose for me to smell.

"Anything for you."

"Thank you."

"You deserve this and more."

"Nothing is worth having without you."

"How did it go?"

"Good. I decided on the color scheme and security setup."

"Do you need me to look over anything?"

"No. I made sure to get people who believe in what I'm trying to do with building. This isn't just a daycare center. I want a place for parents to know their kids are a priority."

"Today is about you relaxing with me."

He flipped me around and massaged my shoulders. I moaned and tipped my head back.

"Was Gaspare asleep when you left?" I asked.

"He's fine. Relax and let me spoil you." He kissed my jaw as his hands roamed up to my neck. Hungry and horny, I faced him again. I looped my arms around his neck and kissed him.

"Before we get into bed, I want to go on deck in my bathing suit."

"I have a bag for you with a change of clothes."

"You"—kiss—"are"—kiss—"amazing." I giggled and patted his chest.

I moved around him to grab the bag off the floor and went to the bathroom to change into the one-piece black bathing suit with a high slit on both sides. I wrapped the shawl around my waist and came out to him waiting for me.

"Ready."

He lifted me in his arms bridal style, and I felt like a school kid with a crush as he carried me out of the bedroom. The yacht captain announced we would start moving out. Axel placed me on my feet and grasped my hand to walk me to the front deck, where a blanket and a glass of apple cider were laid out.

"What made you decide on a boat ride?"

Axel picked up the bottle and poured a small amount for him and me before replacing it in the ice bin. "A small celebration of us. I know my schedule will get hectic with the meeting with the mayor. I never want us to get off track."

I clinked our glasses. "Promise?"

"Promise, baby." He leaned in and took my lips in a soft kiss.

"Beautiful out here." I looked around at the backdrop of New York and felt content.

"Our new normal."

"New normal."

Axel pulled out his phone and showed me a few pictures of Gaspare making different faces.

I laughed. "He's your twin." I took the phone out of his hand.

"Spoiled like his momma."

"Next time, we have to bring him out here."

"Him and the new baby." He placed a hand on my stomach and I rested my hand on top.

Axel let me lean back against his chest and we watched a few young people jump off their boats. The sun would go down in a few hours. I locked our hands together and kissed the back of his palm.

My stomach grumbled. "I'm hungry."

"Sandy made all your favorites." Axel helped me to stand.

I wrapped my arms around his waist and we went to eat.

"We need to make sure we do this once a month," I said as Axel pulled out my chair.

He winked at me. "*Mi amore.*"

We spent the afternoon laughing and reflecting on how much we'd overcome. He'd gone from my best friend to my go-to person, no matter the situation. I believed this was what love was truly about.

Chapter 21

Axel

I had the entire world in my hands with a beautiful wife, a son, and a new baby on the way. When Gigi decided to retire, I supported her and knew how strongly she wanted to have the family business under the leadership of someone she trusted who would carry on Laurent's legacy.

"So, there'll be two kids running around the house soon," Turin joked.

"You know, she started acting weird. I felt she was off, but never imagined she was pregnant."

"I could tell she didn't want to give up."

"I'm glad she didn't. She's pregnant again, and this time I won't be out of the picture in a hospital bed for months on end.

"Bro, she just gave birth," Turin said.

I chuckled. "I missed too much time. Had to play catch up."

"I know she's pissed at you. After she gives birth, let her relax for at least five years before you get her pregnant again."

"She's talking about her charity work and opening her business. The more time she spends on building a business and kids, the better. I think we'll both be occupied."

Turin laughed. "Well, let's go in and handle this business. If I get you back to your pregnant wife in one piece, she won't kill me."

"I missed so much being in a coma. I'm gonna make sure I put her first, and my son is why we're here in Chicago."

Almost all the threats had been straightened out. The bigger problem was the one I was looking at right now, sitting outside Mendoza's home. The minute it was taken care of, we could get back home on our private plane.

The chief set Raymond up with internal affairs on bogus charges. He'll be back on desk duty for a while. I planned to put a tail on him.

Mendoza was another story. I wanted to see his eyes when I killed him.

The compound doors flew open once we turned the power off. Luck was on our side with them living out in the middle of nowhere. No neighbors to see us creeping around in the middle of the night. Turin had some men come through the back, and we approached from the front. We had a layout of the floor plan to get to his room. I screwed on the silencer and crept up the stairs to the bedroom on the right. The guards were dead out front at the gate, and the security cameras had been scrambled to replay the night before, for when the police investigated.

"How many cameras?"

"Counted three, all running on repeat," Turin relayed.

"Let's go."

I pushed the door open slowly and saw Mendoza and his wife asleep in bed. I tapped the gun against his cheek and he opened his eyes.

"Oh my god!" his wife screamed as Turin dragged her out of bed. "Please don't kill me."

"Shut up. Do you know who I am?" I removed my mask.

Mendoza's eyes ballooned in fear.

"You thought I wouldn't come."

"You don't understand. This is business," he murmured.

"Mendoza, you disrespected my wife."

"We can work something out."

I chortled. "Too late."

"Please! I don't know what my husband does for work," his wife begged.

"Shut her up."

Turin shot her in the back of the head.

"My wife!" Mendoza screamed and tried to scramble to her dead body.

I shoved him back against the headboard. "An eye for an eye, Mendoza."

Mendoza tried to reach for his gun on the side table. I hit him with the butt of my weapon and pulled him out of the bed.

"Please, don't kill me. I will do anything you want! I'll give you Chicago."

"Already have Chicago. Everything you own will be transferred to us. Here, type in your code."

His brow dipped in confusion.

"You won't need the money where you're going. Look at it as a donation."

"Then I live?"

I wiggled the phone in his face. "No."

"I am the head of the Mendoza Cartel. Kill me and nothing will move in Chicago or with the Casella family."

"Casella won't be happy with you anyway because of your ties to getting Dario killed."

"Fucking son of a bitch. You killed my wife."

"This is business."

"I have people who will avenge me."

"Should have thought of that before you went against my family and me." I shoved the phone in his chest, pushed the gun to his temple. "Transfer all of your money to that account. Now."

He typed in his information and dropped the phone on the bed. Turin picked it up and confirmed with a nod.

"At least you'll be buried. Unlike Dario." I pulled the trigger.

Turin and I ran out of the house and jumped into the car to head to the airport, leaving the cleanup team to remove all traces of evidence.

* * *

I slept deeply on the return flight and fell into bed next to a sleeping Gigi as soon as I got home. I woke the next morning and turned over in bed, smiling when I saw my son and wife staring at me.

"Did you get him from bed?" My voice was groggy as I rubbed his hair.

"He was crying, so I brought him in here."

I kissed the back of his hand. "Gaspare likes to sleep with us too much."

"Where did you go last night?"

"Handled some loose ends. I think it is time for a little vacay to Italy. Maybe we'll tour Europe.

"I'd like that," Gigi said. "Ebony cooked breakfast. You want to go down?"

"Not hungry. I want to stay like this forever."

"We can't stay up here forever, sleepy pants." Gigi tapped me on the nose.

Being the Boss now took priority over being the Enforcer, and I had to delegate some things to other soldiers.

"Now that I'm pregnant again, I just want to be a mom and a wife. I want to enjoy my pregnancy without stressing over stuff that pertains to the cartel. I don't want to be always looking over my shoulder for someone trying to kill us."

"I'm all for that. Whatever makes you happy."

"Hard to cope with knowing Dario and my mother killed your parents."

"We'll leave the past in the past."

"I can go for that."

She placed Gaspare on top of the bed. I stood and went into the bathroom to freshen up. A huge weight lifted off my shoulders as I stared at the man in the mirror. I'd become a husband, father, and cartel Boss in a matter of months. It could be overwhelming, but seeing the two most important people right next to me smiling and happy gave me strength to do what Laurent Carrington trained and mentored me for, what I was ready for. To be a leader.

I finished with my shower and grabbed clean pants and a shirt. I kissed Gigi as she stood with Gaspare and passed him over to me.

"We should go to the beach today."

I turned back to look at her. "We haven't taken Gaspare to the beach."

"No, but I want to take him to the one back home."

I paused. "Italy."

"Yes. What do you think?"

"Right now?"

"Please? We can be back in the states in a few days. I want him to know his family history."

I hadn't thought about Gaspare knowing where his parents come from. Maybe I'd blocked out that part to focus on what I could control. "Pack a few bags, and I'll call the pilot."

"You make me happy."

"That's my job."

She grinned and turned to go back upstairs to get things together. I went into the kitchen and grabbed a bottle for Gaspare and took a seat to feed him and me. Ebony talked on and on about Gaspare and his feeding habits.

A few minutes later, Gigi came into the kitchen with a phone to her ear. "We'll be in Italy for a few days."

"Who is that?"

Gigi covered the receiver with her hand. "Janice and Sabrina on three-way."

I should have known she would be on the line with those two. Once they met a year ago, they became a sisterhood.

I removed the bottle from Gaspare's mouth and burped him. Placing him in his chair, I picked up the house phone and made arrangements for the flight.

* * *

Italy

The condo looked the same from when we left it a year ago. I still kept cameras and a detail on the place for security, but being back here came with memories of the first time Gigi came to my place and spent the night.

She sat on the couch and covered up with a blanket. The flight had been long and Gaspare's crying had kept us awake. We finally got him comfortable in the guest room that would become to his room while we were here. All it took was money and a phone call to get what you wanted.

"Are you going to call a meeting with Casella and the other families while you're here?" Gigi asked.

I stood at the large window in the living room and stared out at the night lights. "No. We're here to show Gaspare our roots and take him to the beach."

Gigi rose from the couch and stood next to me. "Never thought we would end up back here."

"You had it in your mind to never come back."

"I truly hated what it represented."

My arm automatically went around her waist, drawing her close. She wanted to go by her family home and I'd tried to talk her out of it, but I supported her choices.

"We need to get going first thing in the morning if you want to check on the place."

"Gaspare will sleep during the drive, so we're good." She dropped the blanket on the couch and went to the bedroom to sleep.

I pulled my cell out of my pocket and dialed Turin's number.

"How's it going?"

"Please! We won't get involved!" a voice pleaded in the background.

"All good over here. How is the family?" Turin asked cheerfully.

"Gigi's in bed and Gaspare finally went down."

"Are you coming to the farm?"

I rubbed my chin. "You have any problems?" I heard a buzzing sound.

"The Carringtons can have all the money. We'll give it all up!" another voice begged.

Gigi asked if I would attend a meeting with the Casella family and bring all five families to the table to negotiate. No longer did I feel the need to include anyone in my decisions. Casella's people were pissed about me taking out their man and had good reason. Now I would wipe out the entire bloodline. As soon as they got back to Italy, Turin had kidnapped them and killed the top Bosses in the family one by one. The territory they owned was now under Carrington rule and soon, every cartel family would know not to play with me.

Turin answered, "No, it was an easy pickup."

"Make sure not to leave anything for a burial." I finished the call, and a smile came across my face. Everything had fallen into place.

I headed to the bedroom and stood in the doorway, watching my love sleep with the covers across her bottom half. She wasn't showing yet, but I wanted to be extra cautious with this pregnancy.

I moved close to the bed and pushed the covers further up her body. I sat on the bed and removed my clothes before climbing in next to her.

Gigi rolled over and reached for me. I took her hand and kissed her palm. "Finally, we have peace."

"My peace has always been with you."

I positioned her so we were spooning and rubbed her stomach. She clasped her hand on top of mine and we fell into a deep sleep.

Epilogue

Gigi

Two years later

I carried Antonella in my arms in the banquet hall and smiled at a few of our close friends and family members I hadn't spoken with in a few years. They'd all come to visit and celebrate the grand opening of my new business.

It had been a gradual change for me to not ask about cartel business. With Axel and Turin managing things, it never popped in my head to question anymore. My days were filled with sippy cups and watching cartoons with the kids.

As soon as the issues were handled with Dario and Hugo, I'd realized I needed to be more intentional with my life and cherish my family, rather than prove I could be the Don of a cartel. As a woman, it was rare to be put in that position, but I learned I didn't need to prove anything to anyone. My kids and husband came first over everything else. They brought me peace and joy every day. Gaspare loved being a big brother to Antonella, and

Axel made it a point to travel less to be here for the family.

Antonella fussed in my arms and wanted to get down and play with the other kids.

"Be good, Nella."

Axel wanted me to pick a location that would be close to our home so I could check on the kids and oversee the business, so I found a new place not too far from the city. We ended up extending our property because I wanted more kids and Axel liked privacy.

"The Aurora Children's Center looks fabulous, Gigi." Janice stood before me with her oldest kids and Sabrina.

"Thank you, babe. I can't wait to get more buildings opened."

Sabrina joked, "That degree came in handy."

I finished online for college. I wanted to tell my kids that their mother, despite everything she went through, had gotten her education. Axel and I debated if we'd allow our children to be in the business, but ultimately it was their decision when they got older. The thought of my daughter being manipulated into an arranged marriage pissed me off. I knew Axel would never entertain the idea whenever he told me about meetings he attended with other made men who wanted to secure a future in the Carrington Cartel.

I smiled as Axel started toward me with the phone glued to his ear and Turin right behind him.

"Remember, you already have two under five years of age," Janice teased.

Axel ended his call, wrapped an arm around my shoulder, and kissed my forehead. "Sorry I'm late."

"You okay?" I brushed a finger across his bottom lip and he smiled.

Antonella rushed over with her arms in the air for him to pick her up. Axel bent and scooped her up, kissing her on the cheek. "Everything is fine."

I poked Axel in the chest. "Turin, is he lying to me?"

Turin raised his hands and smirked.

Axel placed his hand on my hip and whispered in my ear. "Be good for me."

Something about his deep voice as his lips grazed my ear gave me the chills.

"Aurora would be so proud of what you've built, Gigi." Sabrina commented.

Aurora was a wonderful house manager, friend, and nanny. I watched more families come in and sign up. The place had a low-cost fee for the application, and all operating dollars came from me and a few donations from friends. Any parent who needed a place to drop their kids off for a few hours while they worked and couldn't afford an arm and a leg could come here.

"We need to plan the next family vacation," Janice said.

I pointed at her oldest kids, and Sabrina's son, AJ. "Before the kids go off to college."

"I hate that I make pretty babies. These little fast tail girls keep calling the house," Janice fussed.

I held in my laughter as she glared at her son across the room talking to some girls who looked older than him.

"I'm glad I don't have that problem." I tickled Antonella's stomach.

Axel placed her on the floor and held out his hand to me. "Come with me."

"Where?"

"A surprise."

"What did you do, Axel?"

He avoided my question and walked toward the door of the building. This man spoiled me so much, I couldn't understand how I got so lucky. He showed me every day that I was priority number one in his life. The breakfasts in bed, the calls throughout the day to check in, and nightly lovemaking showed me a side of Axel I never knew existed when he was my bodyguard. He had always stayed quiet and avoided my questions.

A few people followed us out of the building, and I told Sabrina to watch the kids for me. We stepped outside and a brand-new Ferrari with a red bow on top sat out front with Carrington inscribed on the side.

"When did you do this?" I covered my mouth in shock.

"I wanted to surprise you and had it in motion for a few months. They call it a push gift," Axel answered.

"Baby, you didn't have to give me a gift. Besides, Antonella's not a newborn anymore."

"I know, but we're making up for lost time after Gaspare was born and doing things differently. So not only did I get you one..."

My brows dipped in surprise as another Ferrari pulled up with Ralfie behind the wheel, this one in white.

"You got me two cars?"

"Turin talked me down from buying you one for every day of the week, so I compromised with two. I want you to know how much you mean to me and make up for the times I tried to push you away."

"Axel, you could never push me away. We've been through difficult times, but how we overcame them is what matters most." I rubbed the tattoos of Antonella and Gaspare on his neck while I kissed him over and over.

"Please break up the love fest. We already have these two barely a year apart," Janice joked.

I couldn't resist my husband and how he made me feel every day.

I moved toward the car, opened the door, and sat in the warm seats, playing with the steering wheel and radio. Even with me being driven around by Ralfie, I found a few times to go out and drive myself, though still with security behind and in front of me at all times. Axel didn't take any chances. Our staff was trained to check all guests who entered our front gate.

I was happy to let go of the past and move toward a brighter future. No more pain or distrust. No more lingering doubts as a wife and mother.

I shut the door and threw myself into Axel's arms, thanking him passionately for each gift. As usual, his hands went to my ass, and I had to pull back and remind myself we had kids with us.

I smiled. "I'm ready for an official honeymoon."

"Your wish will be granted, Mrs. Bresciani."

"I'm thinking of the Dominican Republic."

"I'll have the plane ready in an hour."

"You spoil me, Mr. Bresciani."

"That's what happens when you claim the most beautiful girl in the world."

* * *

I hope you enjoyed Gigi and Axel's story. Check the sneak peek of **"Achille Cartel"** on the next page. Follow my standalone, opposites attract, age gap, military romance **"Exposed"** https://books2read.-com/u/bQyYZe. Are you a fan of sports romance? Then download one-night stand, billionaire romance "**Refuel**" https://books2read.com/u/boDyDA. Also, follow it up with workplace, sports romance "**Pressure**" https://books2read.com/u/3Ly1rz. If you love romantic comedy, fake relationships, enemies to lovers, find it here, "**Something Gained.**" Click the link here https://books2read.com/u/baGLYy. My stories of friends finding love started with the Heart of Stone series that includes a host of characters and family. "**Broken**" book 1 Emery and Jackson a sports, one night stand, workplace romance is here: https://books2read.com/u/3LoelX

Then you can continue with a fun side story of Emery and Jackson with "Valentine's Day short here: https://books2read.com/u/4jAypY

Jordan, her best friend's story, continues here in "**Rebirth**" book 2 a single dad, widow billionaire romance here: https://books2read.com/u/ba2OMx

* * *

Please also check out a second-chance workplace romance here, "**Renew Book 4**" https://books2read.-com/u/4NXyPG with a host of characters intertwined.

Follow Desiree and Gabriel in **"Temptation"** a standalone contemporary, sports, curvy girl romance. Check it out here https://books2read.com/u/mle1Vv

Check out dark mafia romance here that started my journey with Antonio and Sabrina in **"Ruthless Book 1"** https://books2read.com/u/4AxKLo

The relationship continues in "**Savage**" book 2 as they get to know each other and their families: https://books2read.com/u/bpED6g

Antonio and Sabrina have more work to do in "**Beast**" book 3 right here: https://books2read.-com/links/ubl/4AxKOd

* * *

Did you know Janice and Carlo have a book? Well grab this dark mafia romance with emotional scars, and betrayal right here: https://books2read.com/u/b6je6M

Any fans of forbidden romance, political? Check out "**Mutual Agreement**" https://books2read.-com/u/mgzzWX a steamy romance. Pre-order the full novel of "**Nasir**" click the link here.

Have you checked out "**She's All I Need**" click here https://books2read.com/u/49lkeW a sports, opposites attract romance. What about dark romance that has everything from steamy romance, opposites attract, suspense, thriller, celebrity, and more "**Stolen Book 1**" https://books2read.com/u/mvZlgV Don't miss the follow up Joaquin and Sofia's story in book 2 "**Saved**" https://books2read.com/u/4DWwLd

The conclusion for Joaquin and Sofia comes full circle in "**Betrayed**" here: https://books2read.com/u/4A5LGp

* * *

Catch up with favorite characters in this holiday short romance which includes spoilers. "**Holiday collection**" here https://books2read.com/u/bzd59G

For small town, single mom stories check out "**Until Seren**a" https://books2read.com/u/mej8vr. Always fun when you love billionaire romances so check in with "**Cocky Catcher**" a sports romance, enemies to lovers here: https://books2read.com/u/bOxNgJ. Some familiar characters show up in "**Bossy Billionaire**" a workplace, enemies to lovers romance here: https://books2read.com/u/mvZoDq

All curvy girl, plus size romance lovers get into "**I Deserve His Love**" a standalone, second chance romance here: https://books2read.com/u/mVrGwP

The fantasy romance readers look no further than a "**Red Light District**" a curvy girl, fling romance here: https://books2read.com/u/m2RQ6G

Reader Questions

1.Do you think Ginerva deserved what happened to her?

2. Should Axel and Gigi wait before having another child?

3.Would Gigi go back on her word and get involved in the business again?

4.Will the Mendoza Cartel come after Gigi and Axel after the death of Hugo?

5.Do you think Axel should retire?

Coming in 2024: Achille Cartel

Coming in 2024: Achille Cartel
Priya

I know my way home. I could get there with my eyes closed. But when I take a shortcut, I end up in unfamiliar territory. What I stumble upon shakes me to my core. Now, I'm firmly in the sights of the Achille Cartel, New York's infamous and brutal mafia family, and Dante, the most sinfully sexy man I've ever seen.

Dante

I call the shots. I make the decisions. I have to deal with the consequences when my guys screw up. The last thing I need is a witness, but now it's happened, it's me who has to clean up the mess. But Priya isn't just any woman. She's sweet, innocent, and too damn irresistible.

What does a mafia boss do with a beautiful school-teacher who was in the wrong place at the wrong time? Can we get this right?

Heart of Stone Universe

Broken 1 Emery and Jackson
https://books2read.com/u/boWPAV
Heart of Stone Book 1.5
https://payhip.com/b/kWg7
Rebirth 2 Jordan and Damon
https://books2read.com/u/ba2OMx
Heart of Stone Book 3.5 Bottoms Up
https://payhip.com/b/HGP1
Reveal 3 Angela and Brent
https://books2read.com/u/31rx9l
Renew 4 Jessica and Joseph
https://books2read.com/u/4NXyPG
The Early Years-A Prequel
https://books2read.com/u/49Zjnw
Ruthless Struck In Love Book 1
https://books2read.com/u/4AxKL0
Savage Struck In Love Book 2
https://books2read.com/u/bpED6g
Beast Struck In Love Book 3

https://books2read.com/u/3LpgdJ
Janice and Carlo Captivated By His Love
https://books2read.com/u/b6je6M
Brutal Struck In Love Book 4
https://books2read.com/u/4NQyE9
Stolen-Fuertes Mafia Cartel Book 1
https://books2read.com/u/mvZlgV
Saved-Fuertes Mafia Cartel Book 2
https://books2read.com/u/4DWwLd
Redemption Struck In Love Book 5
https://books2read.com/u/b5kZ8O
Betrayal- Fuertes Mafia Cartel Book 3
https://books2read.com/u/4A5LGp

About the Author

Chiquita Dennie is an author of Contemporary, Romantic Suspense, Erotic and Women's Fiction.

Chiquita lives in Los Angeles, CA. Before she started writing contemporary romance, she worked in the entertainment industry on notable TV shows such as the Dr Phil show, Tyra Banks show, American Idol, and Deal or No Deal. But her favorite job is the one she's now doing, full time writing romance.

A Best-Selling Author and Award-winning Filmmaker, her first short film "Invisible" was released in Summer 2017 and screened in multiple festivals and won for Best Short Film. She also hosts a podcast that showcases the latest in Beauty, Business and Community called "Moscato and Tea." Her debut release of Antonio and Sabrina Struck in Love has opened a new avenue of writing that she loves.

If you want to know when the next book will come out, please visit my website at http://www.chiquitadennie.com, where you can sign up to receive an email for my next release.

What's Next?

Want to know what happens next?

Follow me on my website to catch the next release.

Reviews are the lifeblood of the publishing world. They're read, appreciated, and needed.

Please consider taking the time to leave a few words on your review platform of choice.

Sign up for updates and sneak peaks at the site below. www.chiquitadennie.com

Acknowledgments

I want to dedicate this to my team that helps me behind the scenes, from my editors, proofreaders, test readers, graphic designers, and especially Crystal. Truly appreciate each of you for keeping me on my toes.

304 Publishing Company

We showcase authors writing African American, Interracial, Women's Fiction, Urban Romance, Erotic, and Contemporary Romance novels. Along with Thriller, Suspense, Poetry, Beauty, and Style Books. Thank you for taking the time out to visit. Join our mailing list to stay updated with new releases and blog posts.

Catalog Releases

Catalog Releases

By Chiquita Dennie:

The Early Years-A Prequel Short Story

Ruthless: Struck in Love 1

Savage: Struck in Love 2

Beast: Struck in Love 3

Brutal: Struck In Love 4

Redemption: Struck In Love 5

Broken Book 1 (Emery & Jackson)

Heart Of Stone Book 1.5 Emery & Jackson A Valentine's Day Short

Janice and Carlo: Captivated By His Love

Rebirth Book 2 (Jordan and Damon)

Temptation

Reveal Book 3 (Angela and Brent)

Cocky Catcher

Bossy Billionaire

Bottoms Up Heart of Stone, Book 3.5 (Jessica and Joseph Short

Love Shorts: A Collection of Short Stories

Stolen: Fuertes Mafia Cartel Book 1

Exposed (Salvation Society Novel)

Saved: Fuertes Mafia Cartel Book 2

Refuel (A Driven World Novel)

Pressure (A Driven World Novel)

Until Serena (HEA World Novel)

Renew Book 4 (Jessica and Joseph)

She's All I Need

Red Light District (A Fantasy Romance Short)

Aydin: TN Seal Security Book 1

Nasir: TN Seal Security Book 2

Betrayed: Fuertes Mafia Cartel Book 3

Something Gained (A Romantic Comedy Book 1)

Torn: The Carrington Cartel Book 1

Claim: The Carrington Cartel Book 2

Thank you so much for reading and if you enjoyed the crazy ride and decide to leave a review, we'd truly appreciate the support.

www.ingramcontent.com/pod-product-compliance
Lightning Source LLC
Chambersburg PA
CBHW011602210726
48287CB00012BC/2716